MW01048042

DEAD MAN AT ANCHOR

And Other Stories

J.E. Rohrer

ISBN 978-1-4116-8833-9

Ordering Information
The Books in the Dead Man series by J.E. Rohrer are
available from lulu.com.

DEAD MAN AT ANCHOR

This book is dedicated to all the homeless people in the world.

CHAPTER 1. ENTER THE WOLF

The dog was loping along behind my car. He was a big fellow, possibly part German Sheppard. His tongue lolled out of the side of his grinning jaws as he easily made the long strides that allowed him to stay near my rear bumper.

The country roads were covered with hard-packed snow. Being a cautious driver, I could not force the car above 40 miles per hour. The wheels would start to feel as if they were losing traction, and I would let the car coast until its speed dropped. Even so, the dog was making me nervous, so I would gently increase speed, only to drop back again right away. My follower seemed to enjoy this game. Perhaps he thought I was doing it for his entertainment, rather than simply out of fear.

And I *was* a little bit afraid. I was taking the back roads up from Illinois, heading back home to Fort Atkinson, Wisconsin. Having left the ugliness of northern Illinois in the wee hours, it was still dark as I was passing through Walworth County. The roads were empty and it seemed that no living souls were within hundreds of miles, except the dog and I, and I wondered about the dog. Did he have a soul? Some spectral aura seemed to radiate from his powerful body. He was so large, I almost wondered if he was a wolf. A few weeks before, the newspapers had reported some movement of wolves into our area. They must have migrated down from Canada.

My companion shifted his position and ran up next to the left side of the car. He looked into my face through the cold window glass with eyes bright and intelligent and fierce. What did he want? I suspected he wanted me to go faster, to give him more of a run for his money. He wanted more of a challenge than I could provide, given my fear of sliding off the road, not that I wouldn't have accelerated to top speed and left him far behind, if only it had been in my power to do so.

The road curved and suddenly approached the outskirts of a small town. The lights were on at a gas station, so I pulled over and parked next to building, which contained a diner as well as a convenience store. I didn't need either gas or food, but some human companionship would have been nice. Looking around carefully, it appeared that the dog-wolf had disappeared. So, I climbed out of my hatchback and went inside.

Three customers were seated at the food counter, sipping coffee and watching me as I came inside. "Mornin'" I said. The waitress behind the counter did not reply, but an older man wearing a furry hat with earflaps gave me a polite response. Seeing the sign for the restrooms, I went through the diner into the convenience store, past another counter where a man in work clothes was standing by the cash register, and into the men's room. Once you are over fifty, the men's room has to be the first order of business in a convenience store.

When I came out of the restroom, the man in work clothes was standing by the glass door that led to the gas pumps, peering out. A small dog was hopping around by his legs, whining. The man opened the door to get a better look at whatever was out there, and the little dog ran out. "Spot!" he shouted. "Come back here!" The little dog did not come back. I went over to where he stood, holding the door open while the frigid February air rushed in. Neither of us noticed the cold, though. We were too intent on piercing the darkness with our eyes. After a few moments of tense silence, we heard a sharp yelp, then nothing.

"Damn!" the man said. "Now I have to get another dog."

"How do you know?" I asked.

"Because this is the third one been killed this month."

"How do you know he's dead?"

"Because the others ran off into the dark just like he did, and there weren't nothin' but a bloody spot left afterwards."

"What do you think is killing them?"

The man looked at me carefully. "Didya seeing anythin' out there when you drove in?" he asked.

"A big dog has been following my car for last ten miles."

The man's face seemed to freeze.

"Does that dog live around here?"

The man pushed past me and returned to the cash register, arms crossed and staring out the window. He seemed to be finished with the conversation.

Back in the diner, I ordered black coffee and perched on a stool. The room was silent. The waitress served me without a word then quietly began cleaning the griddle. She did not offer me a menu. The men at the counter sipped their coffee and stared at the counter. I didn't take it personally; Midwesterners don't feel a need to fill a silence with words. In fact, there is something companionable about men sharing a silence.

By the time my cup was empty, the darkness outside was beginning to lift. "Well, guess it's time to hit the road," I said, to nobody in particular. The fellow with the floppy-eared hat stirred himself enough to ask, "Did you come over from the interstate?"

"Yep."

He looked at me expectantly, waiting for more.

"Not many people out this morning," I said.

He seemed to tense up a bit. "Not many people?"

"Saw a big dog. He chased the car awhile."

"Oh? Where did he drop off?"

"He didn't. He followed me right up to this place."

All eyes were on me now. I dropped a dollar on the counter, then zipped up my coat. "He was a big fellah," I

3

said. Wrapping my scarf tightly around my neck, I added, "He looked almost like a wolf."

Opening the door, I threw back the words "Have a nice day," but the diners couldn't have heard me because the waitress dropped a glass just as I left the place. Maybe it was the coffee pot. Whatever it was, it made a heck of a loud noise.

As I was opening the car door, a grungy-looking man walked up. "You going north?" he asked. I looked him over carefully. Normally I don't pick up hitchhikers, but it was cold and the guy did not have a coat, just a dirty black sweatshirt. He had no hat or gloves. And that big animal was around somewhere.

"Yep," I replied. "Hop in."

It only took a moment to leave that little town behind. The hitchhiker sat quietly, gazing out the window at the passing snow-covered fields. Out of the corner of my eye, I could see that he was very dirty. His hair was matted and he had a bushy beard that appeared to be filthy. He stank, and I started to worry about what kind of marks he would leave on the upholstery.

He saw me looking at him, and gave me an open-mouthed grin. His teeth were large and yellow, with long incisors.

Startled, I felt the need to say something. "Where you headed?" I asked.

"No place in particular."

I wondered if he was homeless. Fishing a business card out of my breast pocket, I handed it to him. "If you need some help, you might call this number." One of my jobs at the time was directing a private foundation that tried to help people who were mentally ill. I didn't want to insult my passenger, but it was not outside the realm of possibility that he might be one of those mentally ill people who roam the countryside, undernourished and unprotected from the elements.

He accepted the card then sat silently for several minutes. Suddenly, he asked, "You think there's something wrong with living rough?"

"If a person wants to live rough and if he doesn't hurt anybody else, then I don't care what he does."

My passenger grinned at me, then asked, "Don't you think there is something evil about lurking in the darkness and living away from people?"

"There is plenty of evil out in the daylight. And evil hurts other people so there is more evil near people than there is away from them."

He pondered this answer for a few miles. Then he asked, "What causes evil?"

"I used to think the love of money and power was the root of evil, but that isn't correct. Some people might say the love of self is the source of evil, but that isn't correct either. The root of evil is self-worship. When a person starts to worship himself, he believes his own gratification is the most important thing in the world. Then, he focuses his energies on getting more wealth and power and he feels entitled to hurt other people. He may not know he is worshiping himself, but his actions reveal what he worships, and the evil person values his own gratification more than anything else."

My passenger seemed to appreciate this little sermon. He chuckled silently, his mouth open and his tongue lolling out. Suddenly, I realized his black sweatshirt had large sticky wet spots on it. His beard was sticky with something wet and his breath could only be described as nasty. His dirty fingernails were crusted with black mud and the knees of his dirty jeans were thick with mud.

The hair stood up on the back of my neck. What I was thinking simply was impossible. This man could not be a transformed version of the dog-wolf. He could not have killed and eaten the little dog back at the diner. Werewolves did not exist.

ENTER THE WOLF

Despite my silent protests, adrenaline was pumping through my body and sweat was pouring from my brow. My passenger seemed to sense my discomfort, because he looked at me sadly, then asked to be let off at the next corner. The intersection was in the middle of nowhere, but he quickly stepped away from the car and disappeared from sight. I sped away. No dog-wolf appeared in my rearview mirror, but still I shook with fear for the next twenty miles.

The sun was up when I pulled into the parking lot of the first convenience store I came to, which was on the outskirts of the town of Whitewater. This place had a submarine sandwich shop on one side. I dropped my exhausted body into a booth. The young man behind the counter gaped at me, then asked, "You okay, mister?"

"Yeah. But I could use some coffee."

He filled a Styrofoam cup and brought it over. "You look like you seen a ghost."

I blew on the coffee to cool it, then took a cautious sip. "No, it wasn't a ghost."

He stopped smiling. "What was it you saw?"

I couldn't tell him the whole story, so I just said, "A big black dog chased the car for a long ways."

The young man paled. "It didn't follow you here, did it?"

That got my attention. "No, I lost it twenty miles back. Why? Have you seen it around here?"

"Not me. But there are stories floating around, about big dogs or wolves. Pets have been disappearing." The young man forced a smile. "It's all just baloney, I'm sure. Still, most people are staying off the country roads at night. Some of the hunters have talked about forming a group to go out and shoot the ....animals. Whatever they are."

I shook my head. "It didn't do me any harm. Scared me, but that was me, not anything it did."

"If it's killing pets, people might be next." The young man was not kidding. I hoped my hitchhiker moved out of the area soon.

CHAPTER 2. ENTER THE COPS

Whitewater was only a short drive from Fort Atkinson, so I arrived home in about thirty minutes. My wife, Betty, had already gone to work, so I had the place to myself. I said hello to the cats, then collapsed onto the bed for a brief nap. The nap turned into a long dreamless sleep. The cats finally woke me in the early afternoon. Bucky was playing with my nose when I fought my way back to consciousness. Reaching for my glasses, my fingers ran into another furry friend; Fritter was on the bedside stand, sitting directly atop my glasses, of course. Fritter was the observer cat. She watched Bucky, Betty and I as we went about our lives. What she found so endlessly interesting was a mystery to me. Watching Bucky I could understand, because he was always doing something stupid. But the two humans led very mundane lives.

Smudged glasses in place, I staggered into the bathroom. After taking care of the essentials, it was time for a shower. As I was dressing, the doorbell rang. I trotted down the stairs from our second floor condo to answer the door. Outside it were a couple of police detectives, Sergeants Schmidt and Broder. I invited them in and led them up the stairs to our living room. After seating them on the couch, I settled into my Morris chair and asked them what they wanted.

Broder cleared his throat as he removed his notebook from the inside pocket of his blazer. His brow knitted as he flipped through the pages. He appeared to be deciding about the best way to begin the interview.

"Hmmm. Professor Schumacher. How have you been?" Broder and Schmidt and I had crossed paths several times in the previous couple of years. However, the two of them obviously were not making a social call. He was fishing for something.

"Fine."

"Are you enjoying life in our fine city?"

"Yep."

Broder seemed to run out of conversational gambits about this time.

"Bill," I said, "why don't you just tell me what's going on."

He looked sheepish, but still refused to tackle the issue directly, whatever it was. "Were you home last night, Professor?" he asked.

"No, I was down in Illinois on business. Just got back this morning. Why do you ask?"

At this point Schmidt lost patience. She was a mean son of a gun, or should I say daughter of a gun? That doesn't sound right, but you get the idea. She was mean and she had always disliked me. I didn't take it personally, preferring to think she disliked everyone.

"Listen, Schumacher," she growled. "We're investigating a murder. Cut the crap and tell us where you were about eight this morning."

"At just about eight I was drinking coffee at a sub sandwich shop inside a convenience store on the edge of Whitewater. The guy at the counter will remember me."

Schmidt snorted, projecting a complete lack of faith in anything I might tell her.

Broder spoke up at this point. "Thanks. We will check that out of course. Just routine."

"It sounds like somebody got killed about eight this morning. Why did you think it had anything to do with me?"

Broder decided to fill me in a little. "Are you familiar with the big antique mall in Milton?"

"Sure. We've been there." My wife Betty was an inveterate shopper. We had been in most of the shops in the area. This particular place was a consignment mall that had hundreds of booths in it, most of them unstaffed at any given time.

"The biggest shop in that mall is the one on the ground floor that sells mostly dishes. I guess you could call it the anchor store of the mall. Do you know the one I mean?" Broder obviously was a little uncomfortable talking about antique dinnerware. I couldn't blame him. But I wished Betty was present because she would have been fascinated.

"Is that the one that is right next to the pop machine and the checkout counter?"

"That's it. Anyway, when they opened the mall this morning at nine, they found a body. The place was a mess; broken dishes and shattered glass were all over the place. The body had been shot in the chest and had only been dead for a short time."

"I'll bet the manager was surprised," I said. "But what made you think of me?"

Broder put down his notebook and studied me carefully. "Because there was a business card in his pocket that had to come from you."

"Oh. I see. Well. That's interesting." My mind was filled with the image of the dirty hitchhiker. He was odd and frightening , but he had not really threatened me in any way. I could think of no reason to kill him, unless you counted fear of the unknown as an excuse for murder.

"What can you tell us about that?" Broder was asking politely, but I could tell that Schmidt was going to jump in with both feet if I didn't give complete answers right away.

"I gave a card to a hitchhiker this morning, not too far from Palmyra. I dropped him out in the country about twenty miles from Whitewater around 7:30."

"He was on foot?" Broder asked, surprised. "How could he have gotten all the way over Milton in the next half hour?"

Schmidt chimed in. "Did you see him get into another car? He had to have a ride, unless he could run thirty miles an hour."

"There were no other cars around when I dropped him off." And maybe he could run thirty miles an hour. But I was not going to say that out loud.

Broder and Schmidt weren't satisfied, but since I could not have been both in Milton and in Whitewater at the same time, they decided to leave me alone. As I escorted them to the front door, I had to ask a couple of questions. "Bill, about that broken glass and the broken dishes. Do you think that happened because somebody was shooting at the poor guy?"

Broder stopped dead and turned to confront me. "Why do you ask that?" he demanded.

"Well, it seemed like a possible scenario. Guy running around the mall, people chasing him and shooting."

Broder regarded me carefully for a moment, then asked, "Any more questions, Professor?"

"Hmm, well, did you find any of the bullets?"

Broder and Schmidt were standing close to me, one on either side. "Why do ask that?" he demanded quietly.

"Just curious. Was there anything unusual about the bullets?"

"Like what?"

"Were they, by any chance, made out of silver?"

Broder and Schmidt froze into stunned silence, then Schmidt shrieked with laughter. "Silver bullets!" she roared. "I told you this guy is a nut!" Both of them were laughing as they went out to their car.

I felt like an idiot, of course. But all that changed when they returned an hour later. The autopsy on the hitchhiker had turned up a silver bullet in his heart.

CHAPTER 3. THE FIRST LITTLE PIG

The business trip to Illinois had come about as a result of a fortuitous combination of circumstances. A large insurance company had a branch office in the town of Jefferson, just a few miles up the road from my home in Fort Atkinson. The branch manager position there had opened unexpectedly and the company needed someone to fill in until they could find a permanent manager. I had no experience in the insurance business, but a friend was the manager of the branch office in Fort and he recommended me for the temporary assignment. The trip down to Illinois had been for the purpose of meeting with the company executives, who decided that I would be perfect for the job because I was unlikely to do too much damage as a temporary manager. For one thing, I did not know enough about the business to make many decisions and, besides, if I tried to make some radical changes, the sales team would just ignore me. It sounded like a pretty easy job. They just needed someone to answer the phone when corporate headquarters called and pass along instructions. Of course, somebody also had to sign the payroll checks and to be present often enough to notice if the secretaries weren't coming to work when they were supposed to.

My first day as a temporary branch manager was the day after the police had grilled me about the silver bullet they found in the homeless man's chest cavity. Understandably, they wanted to know how I had guessed that the bullet would be silver. I had no choice but to tell them the whole story. Fortunately for me, they assumed that the hitchhiker was not a werewolf and that I was just over-imaginative to the point of being hysterical. They were more interested in the information about the possible formation of a vigilante group. When we parted company, Schmidt and Broder were planning on investigating the possibility that the vigilante group was as nutty as I was and therefore felt compelled to use silver bullets on homeless vagabonds whom they believed to be werewolves in disguise. This theory fit the facts as well as any I could dream up, so I wished them luck.

At six that morning I rolled out of bed, put on the coffee, and jumped in the shower. Betty was slower to reach consciousness, but we had worked out a routine for handling that: by the time I got out of the shower, the coffee would be ready. I would bring the paper and a cup of hot coffee, and she would, groaning, drag herself into the semblance of a sitting position. After about thirty minutes, Betty would realize that Bad Boy Bucky, the Terror of the Condo, was batting her nose around with his paws. If Bucky did not do this, Betty would awaken even more slowly. I would be in the other room checking for new email messages on the computer, with our other cat on my lap. When I could hear Betty complaining to Bucky, I knew progress was being made.

"Bucky! Stop that! You are a bad cat today. Get your paw out of my mouth!" Bucky was good at his job, and he loved his work. You had to admire that kind of dedication to duty.

Fritter was just the opposite. She would sit on my lap for her morning petting. She only allowed petting in the morning. If she did not get her pets, she would become depressed. Even so, she never demanded petting. Instead, she would come up to the office chair and look at me until I picked her up. That cat lacked assertiveness. Bucky, on the other hand, had a double dose.

Offering to refill Betty's coffee mug usually brought the same response: "No, thanks. I have to get up." She would say this with as little movement as possible, her head lolling to one side and her arms slack at her sides. Betty looked a lot like a rag doll for the first hour of each day. When she judged that she had stretched time out as much as possible, she would stagger into the shower, dress, and rush out to work. Generally, she did not have time to eat anything and would be starved by lunchtime. Betty would be seeing patients all morning and would be in too much of a rush to stop for lunch, so she would grab a triple mocha cappuccino grande with whipped cream and almonds on top, then jump back into her duties. By evening, she would be exhausted and starved. Of course, getting up five minutes earlier would have prevented some of this discomfort, but Betty's motto was "never do now what you can put off for five minutes." My motto was "do everything ahead of time so you don't have to worry that you won't get it done." To this day I can't say which approach reflected the higher level of mental health. Okay, maybe it's obvious; Betty was less anxious and compulsive, so she won the mental health derby. But I had time for a piece of buttered toast, which had to win me some points.

Pouring the last of the pot into my special Super 8 travel mug (you could get free refills if you stopped into a Super 8), I jumped into my hatchback and headed north on Highway 26. Jefferson was not a big town, so it was easy to find the branch office; it was right on the main drag across from the city building.

Parking in the lot behind the building, I walked in the front door and up to the receptionist.

"May I help you?" she asked. It was eight o'clock, but she did not look bright eyed and bushy tailed, the way a receptionist should. I wondered if she wasn't at her station a little earlier than usual because she had been told that the new supervisor was scheduled to arrive that morning. If so, she was playing her role carefully, not letting on that she already suspected who was waltzing in the door at eight sharp.

"Hi. I'm Ed Schumacher." I stuck out my hand and flashed my cheeriest grin. She forced a weak smile in return, ignored my outstretched hand, and pushed a button on the phone.

"Mr. Schumacher's here," she said, to the unseen person on the other end of the extension. "Brandi will be out in a minute," she said, in a monotone.

We stood there staring at each other for a few seconds. Noticing that her nameplate said "Wilma," I attempted to make small talk.

"You must be Wilma."

"That's me."

"Have you worked here long?"

"Coup'la years." Wilma's eyes strayed over to a women's magazine that lay beside her typewriter. I must have interrupted her in the middle of an exciting story.

At this point a tall young woman, perhaps thirty years of age, opened the door of one of the offices and emerged. She pushed her hand out at me and said, "You must be Mr. Schumacher. I'm Brandi Wilhousen, the office manager."

"Nice to meet you."

"Why don't you come into my office and sit down so I can give you a quick briefing."

"Sure thing."

Brandi had a corner office with windows on two walls. A couple of nice prints decorated the place and a large plant was on a stand by the door. Her desk was covered with a walnut veneer and a state-of-the-art computer rested on it.

"Nice office," I offered.

"Thanks." She seated herself on a leather desk chair then slid a typed sheet of paper across the desk toward me. "This is the list of sales reps with their cell phone numbers. You won't need to call them. They are out on appointments with clients this morning. Most of them will be in the office this afternoon. You can meet them then."

THE FIRST LITTLE PIG

Brandi stood up. "Well, that just about covers it. I'll show you the branch manager's office."

She whizzed past me and walked quickly to the back of the office suite. The manager's office was sparsely furnished. The computer looked to be outdated, the desk was metal, and somebody had switched office chairs. I was pretty sure the previous manager had not used a secretarial chair.

Brandi switched on the light, waved at the desk, and said breezily. "Here ya go. Let me know if you need anything." She turned to go, but I held up my hand.

"Hang on a second, Brandi. You're going too fast for me."

She froze in the middle of her escape, a quizzical and guarded expression on her face.

"First," I began, "I'll need a different chair." I locked stares with her. "You can find a better one than that."

Brandi nodded grudgingly.

"Second, I'll need to see the reports you supply to headquarters. After I look at them, I'll need you to explain them to me."

Brandi said nothing; she didn't have to because the irritated look on her face said it all.

Five minutes later I was ensconced on a better chair and buried under a pile of reports. Happy as a clam, I went to work and she went back to her office, her back rigid. My mind was filled with relief at the thought that this job was only temporary. Firing people is never fun and it looked like whoever took over this office permanently should consider getting rid of dear old Brandi. The woman had an air of extreme competence, but she also seemed to resent having a supervisor.

The office reports were interesting. Not knowing anything about how insurance offices were supposed to look, I was relieved to notice that benchmark information was provided that allowed me to compare 'our' office to others in the company. Our sales revenue per sales representative was about half of the company average. On the other hand, turnover in the sales and office staff was non-existent; people seemed to like their jobs. The salaries of the secretarial staff and office manager, divided by the money paid to the sales reps, was the highest of any branch office in the entire company. In other words, the overhead was sky high.

About the time I figured all this out, the sales reps started straggling into the office. I could hear them joking around in the break room, so after it sound like a good crowd had accumulated, I went in and introduced myself. Three reps were there: Jerry, a smiling young black man with a nice suit; Ann, a middle-aged woman who looked to be your standard Wisconsinite of German heritage; and Will, a kid with a goofy grin with a crooked tie and a shirt that hung out of his pants in the back. They all gave me a warm welcome. We filled our coffee cups and sat around the lunch table for a little chat.

The reps told me a bit about the history of the office, including how long each of them had been there. They all praised Brandi and stressed how indispensable she was.

"She seems like a very competent individual," I offered.

"She's great," Ann gushed.

"Very smart," I said.

"She really takes care of us," Will gushed.

"She doesn't miss much," I observed sagely.

"Smart as a whip," Jerry said quietly. He wasn't gushing. In fact, he looked as if he could tell I was faking it a bit.

"Hey, Ed, how long do you think you'll be with us?" Will broke in.

"Heck if I know. How long did it take them to hire my predecessor?"

"Geeze, a long time. Dave started this past summer. We had a temp for about three months before that, didn't we?" Will turned to the others for confirmation.

"That's right," Ann confirmed. "Dave started in July. The temp manager was here about three months. Before that we had Bill; he was here for six months. The guy before that was here about four months."

"Wow. You sure go through a lot of managers around here."

"Yeah, I guess so," Will said. "But none of them ended up like Dave did." The room grew silent.

"What happened to Dave?"

"They didn't tell you?" All three of them were shocked.

"Not a word. They just said they had an unexpected vacancy."

"That's one way of putting it," Jerry said with a snort.

Ann took pity on me. "Dave was killed in his home just a week ago."

"'My God! Did they catch the killer?"

"Not likely," Will laughed.

"Why aren't they likely to catch him?"

"Not him, it." After Will made that remark, the room grew silent.

"Don't be silly, Will," Ann said. She looked distinctly uncomfortable.

None of them appeared to be willing to explain any more about poor Dave's demise.

"Okay, you guys," I pressed. "You can't leave me hanging like this."

Jerry was the one who told me the story. Apparently, the police report said that Dave had been killed by a wild dog. No one could figure out how the dog had gotten into his house or where it went afterward. Since rumors had been floating around for weeks about werewolves in the area, the local wags had decided that Dave was killed by a werewolf.

"Well, I'll be darned," I said. "That's amazing."

Ann nodded vigorously. "It's the strangest thing that has ever happened around here. I don't believe in werewolves, of course. But just in case, I have a gun under my pillow. You just betcha."

"Is it loaded with silver bullets?"

Ann's mouth dropped open. She slowly stood up. "I have to go out for awhile. I'll be back later."

Will started laughing. "That big bad wolf huffed and he puffed and blew down the little pig's door, then he ate him up." He cackled gleefully at his own humor. When the door slammed behind Ann, he was brought back to reality.

"Where do you suppose she's going?" he wondered.

Jerry just shook his head. "Where do you think she's going? To the gun shop, of course."

"Aw, they don't sell silver bullets," Will guffawed.

Jerry just stared at him until he shut up. "They did last week when I bought mine," he said. Will's eyes bugged out.

Then he grabbed his coat and ran out after Ann.

CHAPTER 4. HE HUFFED AND HE PUFFED

Betty was already home when I pulled into the garage after my first day as a temporary manager. Her little hybrid was squatting in its place in the garage, melting snow dropping off onto the garage floor. Its engine made a ticking noise as it cooled down.

Trudging up the stairs to our living room, I was happy to find her ensconced in her recliner, paging through a catalogue. Betty loved catalogues. What some people might have regarded as junk mail, Betty thought was the most exciting kind of correspondence. She often said the catalogue people loved her, because they always sent her special offers. They probably did love her, considering how much she spent on mail orders.

"Do you think I need new pajamas?" she asked.

"Nope."

"How can you say that?"

"How many do you have?"

"That's not the point. See these pajamas right here? The picture on the right—aren't they beautiful?"

I gave up. "Yes, they're beautiful. You should buy them."

"Do you really think so? You're not just saying that?"

Of course I was just saying that. But why spoil her fun? She knew I was just playing the role she wanted me to play.

"They would be fun to take off," I said, with a leer.

"Oh, you're just being a man. If I took them off, I would get cold. These are great pajamas because they would keep me warm."

"Let's compromise; you can wear the top all night long."

"Oh, you're impossible," she complained with a smile. Then she changed the subject. "How did your new job go today?"

"Fine. Nice people. Laid back. They don't make a lot of money for the company, but so what; the company probably makes plenty of money."

"How did they feel about having a new manager?"

"They're used to it. They seem to get a new manager every three or four months."

"Why so many?"

This made me hesitate. "Well, I'm not sure why most of them left. But the last one was eaten by wolves."

"Eaten by wolves! Come on, what really happened to him?"

"Ok, maybe it was only one wolf. And maybe he wasn't entirely eaten. But he was killed by what the police call an unidentified dog. The gossips in Jefferson say it was a werewolf."

"A werewolf! You get yourself into the strangest situations." Betty sat up straight in her recliner. "How do you know you won't be the next one who gets eaten by a wolf? You quit that job right now! No wonder the company was so eager to hire you!"

"Wait a minute—are you saying they only wanted me for the job because they didn't want any of their good managers to be eaten by a werewolf?"

She didn't back off even a little. "That's right. You were expendable because you don't work for them. You call them up right now and quit that job."

"Now hold on a minute. Jefferson has several thousand people living in it. The chances of the wolf picking me to snack on are very slim. Besides, it only kills people at night. Since I'm here at night, it's sure to eat someone else."

Betty was not convinced. "Are you sure about this?" she demanded.

"Completely sure. Besides, the werewolf is dead."

"Dead? You said the police never found the animal that did it."

"That was the Jefferson police. But a werewolf was killed in antique mall in Milton yesterday morning, while I was driving back from the job interview in Illinois."

"What? How do you know that? Besides, there is no such thing as werewolves. You are making all this up."

"How could I make up something like this? It's true; the police came over yesterday morning after I got home and talked to me about it."

"The police came here yesterday while I was at work and you didn't tell me about it? Why didn't you tell me?"

"Because it would have scared you for no reason. You're a Worry Wart, you know."

"I am not!"

"Yes, you are. You are a Worried Wanda."

"I am not! And where do you get these strange names?"

"They were the names on some of the cards in the Old Maid game we had when we were kids, I think."

"Old Maid? You can't say that."

"Say what?"

"Old Maid. It's sexist. And you're changing the subject.

"What was the subject?"

"The stupid story you told me about a dead werewolf and the police coming here yesterday while I was at work. You start at the beginning and tell me the whole thing."

So I did. When it was finished, Betty just glared at me.

"Is that all clear now?" I asked her.

"What is clear is that you have no regard for my feelings at all."

"Why do you say that?"

"If you cared about me, you wouldn't give rides to werewolves."

"But I didn't know he was a werewolf!"

"And you still don't, because there is no such thing as werewolves!"

"Then I guess I'm not in trouble, am I?" But apparently I was, because Betty stomped into the bedroom and slammed the door.

Once again, a husband faced the age-old dilemma: how to get out of the doghouse. For any male reader who is not yet married, let me explain a fundamental fact of life to you: you will be in the doghouse with a certain degree of regularity. The first five hundred or so times it happens, you will think you are on the verge of a divorce. You will feel terrible. You will wonder if you really are a big jerk. However, after a few years, you will realize that you are looking at the doghouse business from a strictly self-centered point of view. Doghouse-dwelling is not about you, it's about *her*. Being in the doghouse does not necessarily mean you are a bad husband. It most certainly means your wife is unhappy. You should be thinking about some way to cheer her up. Don't make the mistake of thinking you can make a woman happy, because that is impossible. Ultimately, her moods are beyond your control. However, you can be sympathetic about her unhappiness. How would you like to be upset all the time by little things like werewolves? Life would be a series of emotional upsets. It would be exhausting. Give the woman a break; she can't help being a nut.

Being experienced about the doghouse business, I did what any seasoned husband would do. I waited about half an hour, then gently tapped on the door. Tap tap tap. No answer. Tap tap tap. "Go away." Tap tap tap. "What do you want?!"

"Would you like some ice cream?"

Silence.

"We could go to Culvers."

Silence.

"The special of the day is bound to be something good."

"What's the special?"

"I don't know. But it's bound to be good."

How could she argue with that? So, off we went to Culvers. The place was only a block from our condo. The ice cream was good, as always, and it improved her mood.

"I'm sorry I upset you."

"I know you are."

"I didn't mean to."

"I know you didn't." Sigh. "You can't help it. But I just wish you didn't keep getting into dangerous situations."

We went back out to the car holding hands.

I wish I could say that the evening ended on that happy note. However, it did not. Long after we had gone to bed, Betty shook me awake. "Did you hear that?" she demanded.

"Hear what?"

"Just listen."

At first there was only silence, then, off in the distance, I could hear what was bothering her. It was a faint howl. I jumped out of bed and put my ear to the window. The howl was repeated.

"Must be somebody's dog," I mumbled.

Betty snorted. Then the howl came again. It was much closer this time. I tried to peer out the bedroom window, but it was misted over. I sat back down on the edge of the bed. The cats were standing stiff-legged in the middle of the bed, their eyes as big as saucers.

"What are you going to do?"

I just looked at her. "You want me to go out there and tell it to shut up?"

"You are not going out there! You stay right here with me."

"Well, I don't know what you want me to do, then. I refuse to call the police and tell them we have a werewolf outside of our door."

Betty frowned. "You know," she said. "We're getting hysterical here. Just because of some silly story about werewolves, we have started thinking a howling dog must be a werewolf. That's ridiculous. We should just go back to bed and forget about it."

We went back to bed, but we didn't forget about it. The dog, or wolf, howled for what seemed like hours. Then it stopped, and we finally fell into exhausted slumber.

The next morning, I walked around the building, looking for tracks. The marks in the snow seemed to be telling me that a dog had circled the building several times during the night. However, most of the tracks were below our bedroom window.

As I was studying the tracks, our downstairs neighbor came out to join me. Emily Eberhardt was a very sensible matronly woman. She would not jump to any hysterical conclusions about werewolves.

"Morning, Emily."

"Good morning, Ed. Or it should be a good morning. After all that noise last night, I'm a wreck this morning."

"Yep, it kept us awake too. This looks like its tracks."

"That must be a very big dog. Those tracks are enormous."

"Yeah, I guess you're right."

"Maybe it's not a dog."

"What do you mean?"

"According to the paper, Canadian wolves have been moving farther south each year. They were down into northern Wisconsin a few weeks ago. Maybe one of them has worked his way this far south."

"I heard wolves never attack people. We shouldn't have to worry."

"That may be so," Emily said sternly. "But what was it doing howling outside our building last night? That's what I want to know."

I   didn't   have   an   answer   for   her.

CHAPTER 5. BANG! BANG!

The snow-packed roads were slick that morning, so I took my time driving to Jefferson. Unfortunately, most of the other drivers wanted to go faster than I, so a long line of cars accumulated behind me. Every now and then one of the pickup trucks would zoom around me, spraying slush in his wake. None of those guys ended up in the ditch, but we passed a couple of their cousins. They must have lost control during the night - after having a snootful, no doubt - because now they appeared to be abandoned and they wore thick blankets of snow.

Drinking to excess was fairly common in rural Wisconsin. Lest you think this problem was limited to under-educated farmers, consider this: the frat houses over by University of Wisconsin-Whitewater were periodically busted for drinking parties. These were not just your usual have-a-couple-of-beers type of party. These parties really crossed the safe-drinking line. You couldn't say the guilty parties were undereducated farmers, though they were no doubt related to some.

It was nearly eight when I arrived at the office. Wilma, our cheery receptionist, had not arrived yet. Brandi arrived at the same time I did, so we exchanged polite greetings. I searched around for the coffee fixings then put the pot on. While I was waiting for it to drip through, I tried to make small talk with Brandi.

"Nice weather we're having."

"Could be worse," she replied guardedly.

"Yep. But I'm glad I'm not homeless."

She laughed. "That would certainly be uncomfortable."

"Does Jefferson have a homeless shelter?"

"There's a house a few blocks from here that will let transients stay for a day or two."

"Sounds like that might be a worthy charity. If they are kicking people out after a couple of days, they must need more space."

Brandi frowned. "The women's shelter is running a fund drive this month, if you're looking for a charity."

"Lots of people care about battered women, but not as many seem to care about the single person who is permanently homeless."

Brandi snorted, whirled around, and went into her office. Apparently I had said the wrong thing.

The coffee was ready, so I filled my cup then went into my own office and sat behind the desk. As the computer was warming up, I wondered what I was going to do all day long. I had finished going through all the reports the day before. Around lunch time, the sales reps would show up. Until then, surfing the Internet seemed like the only activity available. My first instinct was to ask Brandi what the previous manager did with his time, but now did not seem like a good time to bother her with foolish questions.

Wanda, our receptionist, arrived about twenty minutes later. She banged around her desk, getting settled in. The phone had rung a couple of times before she arrived. The calls were for our sales reps. I handed her the message slips, which seemed to irritate her. She did not appear to be a morning person. Maybe it was my imagination, but I couldn't help suspecting that calls coming in before nine would have gone unanswered, as a general rule.

"Do you get many messages for the reps?" I asked cheerfully.

"No. People generally call the reps directly."

"What if they are new customers and don't have a rep yet."

"The reps are listed in our ad in the yellow pages. Anybody can pick a name out and call directly."

"You mean you don't help them if they call the general number?"

By this time Brandi was standing behind me. "The reps all have voice-mail. Callers don't need to bother the front desk."

"Customers might prefer to talk to a human being."

"That's not how we do it."

"Who decided that?"

"It's the policy." Brandi gave me a flat stare, straight between my eyes. She was daring me to challenge her on this.

"I wonder if the other branch offices do it this way," I said, with my best thoughtful expression. Then I went into my office, closed the door, and called my friend Steve Winters, who managed the branch office down in Fort Atkinson. He was the one who recommended me for the job in Jefferson.

"You bastard! What have you gotten me into?"

He laughed. "What are you complaining about? I handed you the easiest job in the Midwest.

"Yeah, if you don't mind being unwanted. These women are hoping I will slip on the ice and be hauled away by EMTs."

"Brandi has a good reputation. Everybody says she holds the place together."

"She does. It's her way or the highway."

"What did you do? Are you stirring up trouble already?"

"I just asked if the receptionist ever answered the phone. Apparently, new customers should feel privileged if they can leave a voice-mail message for a rep. Talking to a human being would be asking for special favors. Is that how you guys do it?"

"Of course not."

"I know it's not. I just called your office and got a cheery 'hello'. If I needed insurance I would buy it from you guys, not this place."

"Ed, I have bad news and good news for you."

"What's the bad news?"

"If you found that kind of problem on your second day, then there is a whole lot of other bad stuff going on that you don't know about yet."

"Great. What's the good news?"

"As long as your office is that rude, my office will get plenty of business."

He was laughing his head off when I hung up on him.

My next call was to Betty's cousin Andrew. We agreed to meet at Bienfang's in Fort Atkinson for a beer after work. Given how well I was doing at the office, I could have left for a beer at ten in the morning and not come back. They would have been glad to see me go.

The sales reps began straggling in around eleven in the morning. Apparently, the dismal weather was putting a damper on their activities. Some of the businesses they dealt with were closed and others were experiencing some absenteeism. Few wanted to talk about insurance.

Consequently, we decided as a group to walk down the street to a local restaurant where we could swill coffee for a long time and shoot the breeze. Working with sales reps was starting to seem like a pretty good life; they were easy going, personable, and willing to talk about anything.

For example, they told me about the previous manager. He had been a divorced single guy who was transferred to Jefferson from Chicago. Needless to say, he did not exactly fit in. He drove too fast, talked too fast, and generally was too pushy. However, he was a good salesman, which meant he was flexible. He was gradually learning how to deal with the locals.

Even so, the team said he was not happy. He would have been fine as a sales rep, but being a manager was difficult because he did not get along with Brandi. As a new manager, he would sometimes come up with ideas for changing procedures. Those ideas had all been tried before and rejected. Brandi did not appreciate boat-rocking, so she froze the guy out. By the time the wolf ate him, he was completely unable to function as a manager. Brandi ignored him, his computer was broken, his telephone stopped ringing, and none of the sales reports were reaching him. He was a very frustrated guy.

After frittering away most of the afternoon, I finally went home. The sun had come out, the snow was melting a little, and I couldn't stand faking it any longer. So I took off.

As I was driving home, I thought about how scary Wisconsin could be. Most of the time, of course, there was nothing scary about the place. The people were nice, the crime rate was low, and anyone with any sense would want to live there. But there was a spooky underside to the place. After all, the state had a lot of forests, and forests can be scary places. If you don't think so, then you have not been out in a forest very often.

One time, when Betty and I were driving back from a visit to the northern part of the state, we stopped into a supper club for dinner. Supper clubs were restaurants frequently found on the byways of the state. This supper club was around Neillsville, if I remember correctly. We enjoyed the usual supper club fare of standard American food, and passed the time eavesdropping on the conversation that was taking place at the next table. Two middle-aged couples were out on a double date. The men were talking about a particular place where they went regularly to cut down red oak.

First man: "Every time I went up there, I felt like somebody was watching me. It gave me the willies. Never felt that way anywhere else. Didn't want to mention it, because it sounded silly. Then yesterday Bill here told me he felt the same way when he went up in that woods."

Bill: "That's right. It's a strange feeling. Like chills down your back. Your hair stands on end."

First man: "Since Bill noticed it too, it must be real."

First woman: "You guys are just making this up to scare us."

Both men: "No, we are not making this up."

Both women: "Yes, you are and it's scaring us so change the subject."

So they changed the subject. Betty and I smiled at each other, then finished our meal. When we were back in the car, she asked me if I thought the men were serious. "They sounded serious to me," I replied.

"Oh, you're just trying to scare me. Now stop talking about it."

So I did.

CHAPTER 6. ED MAKES A LIST

After pulling into the garage when I had returned home from Jefferson, I trotted up the stairs to the condo, took off my sport coat, and put on my smoking duds. I was a pipe smoker, and I did not smoke in the house. That meant I needed special clothes. After all, it was winter in Wisconsin.

No, I was not foolish enough to smoke out in the snow. Instead, a chair, space heater, and lamp were set up in the garage. Even with those preparations, it was necessary to wear a down vest, a warm coat, a scarf, and cowboy hat. The most important piece of equipment was Bucky, the fatter of the two cats. He liked to sit on my lap while I smoked. Fat cats make better lap warmers, you know.

Pipe smoking was my opportunity to review events and try to make sense out of them. The awkwardness at the office was not my concern; that job was temporary and there was no point in wasting much brain power on it. The werewolf problem was more interesting. Not being able to think without making notes, I reached for my handy mechanical pencil and jotted down the following questions:

1. Were the werewolves real?

2. If not, what was going on?

That was a good place to stop and scratch my head. This was possibly the dumbest set of questions I had ever written. Werewolves did not exist! For the sake, of sanity, I would just have to assume that the werewolves were not real. Another explanation had to be found for the strange series of events.

That thought gave me an idea. Instead of writing questions, I should begin by listing the events that were bothering me.

3. A strange guy rode with me in my car
4. People in the area were claiming to have a werewolf infestation; pets were being killed
5. The guy who hitched a ride with me ends up dead at the anchor store in the antique mall
6. He was shot with a silver bullet
7. The manager of the branch office was killed by a wolf or a wild dog
8. A noisy animal was howling outside of our condo the night before.

Making this list was very helpful. Right away I knew what I should be doing. My immediate challenge was to develop a theory that fit the facts listed. First off, I could pretty much assume that the dead man at the anchor was killed by the local vigilante group that had taken upon itself the responsibility for wiping out what they believed to be a tribe of werewolves. The kid at the convenience store near Whitewater had told me that a group of hunters was going to do just that.

The dead pets might be explained by the migration of wolves down from Canada. That theory also could explain the howling in the night. However, it did not explain why the wolves had chosen to howl outside our window, rather than somewhere else. Unfortunately, the Canadian wolf theory seemed nearly as fantastic as the werewolf myth.

If Canadian wolves were not the problem, then what theory could compete with the local werewolf myth? Pets had been killed and so had a branch manager. These deaths were real. The howling outside of the condo was real. I would need another theory other than werewolves, but the explanation was not jumping up and offering itself for inspection.

At that point, I had to give up. No brilliant insights were emerging. But I was sure the truth would somehow be revealed. And, somehow I knew that truth would turn out to be stranger than fiction.

That evening, Andrew and I met at Sal's for a beer after dinner. Naturally, I told him the whole story about the werewolf myth. Naturally, he thought I was nuts. "Werewolves!" he laughed. "Ed, you have had some strange ideas, but this is the weirdest one of all. Werewolves! I don't believe it."

"I don't either. That's why I called it a myth. Unfortunately, a bunch of rednecks with guns are taking it seriously. They killed some poor homeless guy because of it."

"Well, okay, I guess I shouldn't laugh. But you sure get yourself into some ridiculous situations."

"How am I in a situation? I'm just thinking about the problem. It's not my problem."

"Oh, yeah? Who has a wolf howling outside his bedroom window? Who is holding down the chair last occupied by a guy who was eaten by a wolf?"

"Now you're sounding like you believe in the werewolf theory."

"No, I don't believe it. But if there was a werewolf in the area, it makes sense he would be following you around. After all, you tend to attract strange characters."

"You're no help at all tonight. Laughing at me won't explain all this. Besides, nobody in Wisconsin is supposed to be in that good of a mood in the middle of the winter. We are supposed to be in the throes of depression due to light deprivation."

For a moment, I hesitated then asked him, "Hey, you gotta new girlfriend?"

"What makes you ask that?"

"Because you're so blasted cheerful, that's why."

"Well, now that you mention it, I do have a hot date this weekend."

"I knew it! Now, can you get your mind off your weekend plans and help me try to figure this out?"

It was hopeless; Andrew could not get serious about anything as trivial as werewolves when he was planning a hot date. I was on my own.

That evening, Betty and I went to bed without mentioning the question we both had in the forefront of our minds: would the howling return? Just after midnight, it did. It jarred me out of an uneasy sleep. This time, Betty did not need to shake me awake. The darn thing sounded like it was suspended in the air directly outside our window.

I rushed to the window and pulled up the blind, but once again it was covered with ice and nothing could be seen. Suddenly a couple of loud noises punctuated the night. Bang! Bang! Pulling on my warmest winter coat, I ran down the stairs and out on to the sidewalk. Emily was standing out in front of her unit, which was directly below ours. She was carrying a shotgun.

"Emily!" I gasped. "What are you doing?"

"We can't have wolves roaming right up next to the building!" she responded. Since she was on the ground floor, I could understand her concern.

"Do you really think a wolf is going to break into your house and eat you?"

"It might!"

"Well, shoot it when it does. But you can't go running around the block in your nightie shooting at whatever looks like it might be a Canadian wolf."

"I can't?"

"If I was having a loud party, would you shoot me?"

"Of course not."

"Well, then why shoot a dog for howling? He's just partying."

Emily paused to consider this argument.

"Emily," I went on. "Would you want other folks running around in the night with shotguns? Somebody might miss and put a load through your bedroom window."

She straightened up at that. "You're right, Ed. Some fool might do just that." She turned to go back inside then stopped. "But I shoot what I aim at. If that noisy animal sticks his head up to my window, he's going to lose it."

"Okay, fair enough. I just hope we don't have any peepers in the neighborhood."

"Serve 'em right," she grumbled, as she went back into her apartment.

For a few minutes, I remained out on the sidewalk. The night had turned silent. Perhaps Emily had scared it off, whatever 'it' was. Perhaps it was out there, watching me. The night air was cold, so I shivered. Time to go back in. And to double-check the bolt on the door.

CHAPTER 7. ED TRIES TO GO GREEN

The next morning, I jumped out of bed with more than my normal enthusiasm. For one thing, the Green Party was having an organizational meeting in the Jefferson library and I planned to be there. Another reason I bounced out of bed with a lot of energy is that Bucky lay down on my chest with his tail end in my face. Talk about a motivator.

Bucky was the bad boy of the household. When he was wound up, he would bounce around the kitchen at a flat run, knocking dishes off the counter tops as he went. He would sometimes bang a door against the wall, just to watch the plaster fall out of the hole the door knob made in the wall. Bang! Bang! Bang! He was clumsy, impulsive, rude, and ate like a pig. On the other hand, he also was very affectionate and would purr loudly when being petted. Our other cat, Fritter, was much better behaved overall. She would sit on my lap in the mornings very quietly, like a well-behaved young lady should. The only bad behavior she was guilty of was a tendency to sharpen her claws on the leather loveseat. As you no doubt have figured out, we spoiled those cats.

When I got to the office, Brandi's SUV was already in its regular parking slot. For the past year or two, critics had been complaining about SUVs, mostly because of poor fuel efficiency. My own beef with them was safety. If people wanted to waste their money on cars that had terrible fuel efficiency, that was their own business. What bothered me was that too many SUV drivers behaved badly when behind the wheel. You often could hear people justify buying a big SUV on the grounds of safety. "Oh, if I get in an accident I want a lot of metal between me and the other car." That was nonsense. If an SUV was involved in an accident, odds were that the SUV driver had caused it by driving too aggressively. Accident rates were high for SUVs. Single car fatality rates were very high for SUVs. If SUVs really were safer than other cars, who could we blame for the single-vehicle accidents? Getting behind the wheel of a powerful vehicle seemed to cause some people to lose touch with reality. Or, perhaps, they naturally wanted to drive too aggressively and they were forced to be more reasonable when driving smaller vehicles. Either way, the SUVs had become a menace on the highways.

I spent the morning ruminating on SUV drivers who were out of control, but did not say a word out loud. Brandi disliked me enough already. Besides, I could not assume she was a bad driver just because she drove an SUV. That would have been negative and judgmental, traits that I had in abundance but worked hard to control.

Around eleven in the morning, I put into motion my plan for solving the werewolf problem. The first step was to call Doc Watson over in Fort Atkinson. Doc Watson was chairman of the board of a private foundation for which I was the titular director. The truth was, all decisions were made collectively and so I did not really direct anything. But it pleased the board to have a director, and I enjoyed the role.

The foundation was created to administer the fortune a homeless man had made on Internet stocks. His will had established a foundation that aided mentally ill people without interfering with their liberty. The board was composed of people whom the deceased gentleman had met during his sojourns as in inpatient in the psychiatric hospital in Madison. They must have composed the most interesting board in the corporate world.

ED TRIES TO GO GREEN

Doc listened patiently while I explained my problem. He agreed to line up a surveillance team that would watch my condo that evening. Not once did he question me about the reality of werewolves. Doc, no doubt, had heard stranger stories. He himself probably had seen stranger things than werewolves several times in his life.

The sales reps were straggling into the office by this time, which caused me to realize that Wilma still had not arrived at work. "Brrr," Jerry said. "It's too darn cold to be running around out there."

""You're right about that." Will agreed.

They seemed to be watching me out of the corners of their eyes, to see if the temporary boss would have something to say about coming back to the office during cold weather.

"You wouldn't catch me out there more than I had to be," I announced. The three reps relaxed and bunched up around the coffee pot.

Ann noticed the cat fur on my blazer. "Oh, do you have cats?" she asked.

"Yep. We have two. They pretty much run the household."

"I have two also. They can be so entertaining."

Jerry shook his head. "Cats entertaining? You must be kidding. They sleep all day long. What's entertaining about that?"

"Oh, you're just not a cat person. You'll never understand."

"I guess you're right. If I had to pay for extra dry cleaning because of cat hair, I would be really irritated."

"Dry cleaning?" I broke in. "Who pays for dry cleaning?"

"You're just kidding," Ann said. "You get your clothes dry cleaned. Don't you?"

"Actually, I don't. Blazers don't get sweaty, so they only need to be cleaned when they acquire visible dirt that can't be washed off with a damp rag. The only stuff I can't get off is the cat hair, and I refuse to pay for dry cleaning just for that. And all my clothes except blazers are wash and wear."

"Wait, a minute," Will said. "I pay a bundle every week for dry cleaning. Are you saying I don't need to do that?"

"No, you don't. Buy wash and wear slacks. When your blazers get wrinkled, throw them in the dryer and the wrinkles will come out."

The room suddenly grew quiet. Brandi was standing in the door, frowning. Apparently, she did not think it proper for the temporary boss to encourage the reps not to dry clean their clothes. When we were all looking at her, she turned and went back into her office.

"Did you see that look on her face?" Jerry asked.

Will grinned at me sympathetically. "You're toast, buddy," he said to me.

"Yes, I'm afraid she's not a cat person," Ann said apologetically. That brought a laugh from all of us. But nobody laughed very loudly.

The Green Party meeting was to be held at five at the library. Being an opinionated guy, I was looking forward to the meeting. I had not voted for either of the two major parties for a long time, and was always in search of a third party that had some good ideas.

When I arrived at the library, I had to ask directions to the meeting at the circulation desk. They sent me to the back of the building, where the magazines were kept. A few seedy looking guys were taking advantage of the free reading material, slouched in easy chairs. Inside the conference room, half a dozen seedy looking guys were grouped around a table, along with a man in a suit, who turned out to be our speaker. After introductions were made, a fellow by the name of Albert began to lecture us. He was a Green Party representative from Madison. Unfortunately, he was focusing on what seemed to me to be theoretical issues. Ecology, proportional representation, and ballot box fraud had him worked up. The possibility of paperless voting incensed him. This seemed a little odd to me. After all, my banking was all done on computers. If they could keep track of money that way, then they should have been able to count votes.

I managed to sit quietly through all this until the speaker got on the subject of the classic zero-growth book "Small is Beautiful" by Schumacher.

"Hang on a second," I broke in. "My name is Schumacher too, you know. The guy you are talking about was my great uncle twice removed. I never met him but those of us who went to college in the seventies know about 'Small is Beautiful' and other classics of the period. That book sits in a place of honor on my shelf at home. But the average voter is not going to care about that stuff. The average voter cares about bread and butter issues. You have not said a word about affordable housing, transportation, or job skills training. Everybody knows the Greens support environmentalism. This is Wisconsin, everybody likes trees, so if you don't get votes, it won't be due to any anti-environmental attitudes. If you don't get votes, it will be because you are not talking about the issues the average person cares about. So, tell us: What do you have to offer the voters?"

Albert was thrown off his patter by my interruption. To give him credit, he rallied pretty well.

"We support national health insurance. Administrative costs and corporate profits are the main reason our health care system is so expensive. Look at the new Medicare drug benefit - drug companies are making a killing on this. Our system has hundreds of private insurance companies, all making profits. They lobby Congress to stop any national health insurance program from being enacted."

"That's right. They do that. Yes, of course, a national program would be better than what we have, though I could quibble with your preference for national health insurance rather than a system that looks more like what the Brits do for primary care. But, as you just said, big business is going to prevent the enactment of any program that will provide universal coverage at an affordable cost. We need an alternative approach."

Our speaker visibly resisted the temptation to ignore the issue I had raised and rush back into his monologue. "What kind of alternative are you talking about?" he asked, forcing a patient smile.

"One of the fundamental realities of our century is that incomes will drop. Young people will find that many jobs have been outsourced to nations where hourly rates are very low and no employee benefits are offered. Sure, some of our young people will end up in corporate jobs with good salaries. But, many will be paid as contractors, so much for completing a job, like house painters. They will feel lucky if they can make minimum wage.

"This means that all the essentials will have to be rock-bottom cheap. Houses, cars, education, and medical care will have to cost far less than they cost now. Americans will have to get reacquainted with ideas like the tiny bungalows of the arts-and-crafts era, the Sears-Roebuck mail-order house, manufactured housing, and row houses. We will need inexpensive small vehicles that are light-weight and fuel-efficient.

"Tax revenues will drop. That means schools will not be able to afford to use old-fashioned face-to-face teaching methods. They can close the high-schools and teach job skills over the Internet.

"In this kind of economy, you can forget health insurance, except for major surgery. Most medical care will become a cash business and it will have to be inexpensive. Doctors will learn to diagnose and prescribe using computer programs, which they can do over the Internet. Your prescriptions will be mailed to you. It will be about as much fun as calling customer service when your computer breaks down, but it will get the job done. People who want to pay a hundred bucks out of pocket will be able to see a doctor face-to-face, but everybody else will use the Internet.

Political parties could offer policies that will smooth this transition. You could say you support a national medical license, so doctors will be able practice on the Internet without worrying about where the patient is located. You could make sure Internet connections are free. You could cut Medicare costs so that young people are not crushed by the taxes that will be required to enable all the Baby Boomers to kick the bucket in a hospital intensive care unit, instead of in a comfortable hospice bed."

The Green Party representative from Madison was stunned. "Ed," he protested. "These ideas of yours have not been evaluated. We can't go off on a tangent this way. Let's get back on track." He consulted his notes. "Oh, yes. Proportional representation. We need one-person, one vote. We need to eliminate the electoral college. We need to break the lock the two major parties have on the political system. In other countries, if a party gets twenty percent of the vote, then they get twenty percent of the seats in the legislature. We need to amend the constitution to give the people a voice."

Blast! He was back on esoteric issues. "All that sounds okay, Albert," I said. "But the average voter knows that over in Minnesota, Jesse Ventura managed to get elected governor without any constitutional amendments. So, it can be done. The Greens could win too, if they would talk about bread and butter issues. For example, what about affordable housing?" And off I went, pontificating about homelessness.

"We do not assure basic housing in Wisconsin. Homeless people live in the snowy woods, huddled over campfires. Unless the ambient temperature is extremely low, they are permitted access to homeless shelters only for limited periods of time. Then, miraculously, they are expected to have landed jobs that will enable them to pay the going rate for rent.

"Unfortunately, many people cannot make the leap from homelessness to self-sufficiency. A homeless person will have to work 40 hours per week at minimum wage to be able to pay rent and buy a few groceries. Of course, if he could hold down a steady job, he probably would not be homeless in the first place.

"Why do we assume that all homeless people only require temporary assistance? Many people just cannot get it together enough to compete in the modern economy. Yet, people should be able to live decently even if the best they can do is to work sporadically in minimum wage jobs.

"A political party should make this problem into an issue. We could solve the problem with no federal money, if we just approached it correctly. Why not let people in search of tax-deductible opportunities for charitable donations buy shares in a trailer which can be given to a homeless person, earning a tax deduction in the process? Local governments or local charities would have to pay the lot rental and utilities, but this is a pretty cheap way to eliminate homelessness. In fact, local government should be able to ask the local utility providers to provide free electricity, water, sewage, and trash pickup to these trailers."

Needless to say, the Green Party stalwarts got tired of me. I had not mentioned a tree or an endangered species even once. They asked me to leave. I didn't blame them; it just wasn't working out between us.

The two street people were still hanging around outside the meeting room when I left. By now, however, both had newspapers draped over their faces. If they overheard my speech, it must have put them to sleep.

CHAPTER 8. THE SECOND LITTLE PIG

Back on the sidewalk, the night air was cold and much fresher than what we were breathing in the library. I drew in a lung-full, letting it out slowly. My pulse began to slow down a bit; the meeting had really gotten me worked up. Apparently, no political party was far out enough for me to be able to join it. I had to face reality; my political opinions were just too nutty for anyone to take seriously. Like most people, I did not trust big corporations and had no confidence in big government. What the government did best was regulatory: regulation of public safety, environment protection, regulation of business practices, and the like. Which political party was the natural home of a guy who trusted neither business nor big government, and who favored government regulation, but was against government spending? None, apparently. This was a sobering thought, but I shrugged off the sense of isolation it gave me and headed back toward my car.

The sun goes down early in the winter, so very little light was left by the time I had covered the first block. My car was back at the branch office, only about ten blocks away, but the winter wind seemed even colder in the darkness than it had during the day. No one seemed to be out and about except me. Probably that meant that everyone else had more sense. Leaving your car ten blocks away in the middle of winter was just plain dumb. I would have kicked myself, except that my butt was too frozen to feel it.

Where possible, I walked down the alleys between streets in an effort to stay out of the wind. With my head hunched between my shoulders and a scarf wrapped tightly around my face and ears, my hearing must have been impaired. How else could the animal have gotten so close to me without my noticing it? My first clue that I was not alone was hearing a growl that sounded as if it was right behind me. Stopping short, I turned to look. This was a reflexive action, and it proves that reflexes are not always the best guide to behavior. Think about it; I was hustling down the alley, heard a growl behind me, then stopped and turned to look. Whatever had been near to me when I heard it growl, was now looking me straight in the eye from a distance of three feet.

Was it a wolf? How would I have known? After all, I had never had the pleasure of meeting an honest-to-goodness real-life wild-and-wooly wolf before. All I could say was this thing was big, furry, and had fangs longer than my fingers. When he opened his mouth, as he was doing at that moment, he had enough room in there to fit in my entire head.

I don't actually remember turning around and starting to run. If it is possible for a man to spring straight up into the air, turn one hundred and eighty degrees, and take ten running steps, all within the space of a second, then that must be what I did, because in the next moment I was running as fast as my ancient legs would take me toward the mouth of the alley. The animal was snarling at my heels. If he had been a bit taller, I could have felt his hot breath on the back of my neck.

Being a guy who believed that walking is the only form of exercise a person needed, I was not a practiced runner. Fear lends wings, making flat feet fleet. Even so, I only made as far as the next street before he brought me down by leaping onto my back. Immediately, I was flat on the ground, holding those fierce fangs a few inches from my throat by gripping the animal's hairy throat, and pushing with all my strength. The coarse fur on its throat was thick and warm. I remember thinking that his pelt would have made a nice coat, if I just had a way of killing the nasty creature.

Suddenly he was off me. He was snarling and leaping at someone else, someone wearing a trench coat. Staggering to my feet, I could see that it was a woman. The beast had her down now, her arm gripped in his fangs. He began shaking his head, seemingly intent on tearing the arm out of its socket. She screamed. I jumped on the monster's back, wrapping my arms around its head. He let go of her arm, and turned his attention to me. Throwing me off his back, he turned and leered. I swear, it looked as though he was thinking, "I'm going to enjoy ripping this jerk to pieces."

Just as he gathered himself to leap, a search light sprang out of the darkness, transfixing the animal in its glare. The monster was momentarily frozen, but moments are brief. He whirled, leapt out of the beam, and disappeared.

The alley was suddenly very quiet. I could feel my breath rasping in my chest, and the exhausted sobs of the woman lying on the ground next to me. Footsteps crunched on the ice and gravel then I heard a voice ask, "Are you okay, Professor Schumacher?" It was Sergeant Bill Broder, of the Fort Atkinson police department. That meant the woman on the ground next to me had to be my old enemy Sergeant Schmidt.

"Yeah, I'm fine. But Schmidt here has been bitten. Better get her some help."

The EMTs arrived shortly. Broder and I sipped hot coffee in the back of their van while they treated Schmidt.

"What brings you guys to Jefferson, Bill?" I asked him.

He shifted uncomfortably. "Mmmm. Police business."

"And it was just a coincidence that you happened to be in the alley when I was there?"

Broder looked out the windows of the van, seemingly deaf to my question.

"By the way, thanks for showing up when you did. I would have been dog food if you hadn't been there."

He finally looked at me directly. "Thanks for helping Schmidt. I saw you jump on that animal when it had her down. That took a lot of guts."

"No problem. Anybody would have done the same." I didn't tell him that if I had known it was Schmidt, I might have had second thoughts about leaping to her defense.

"It was nice thing to do and I want you to know I appreciate it. By the way, it looks like you have a scratch on your neck there. It's bleeding a bit."

The EMTs slapped a band aide on my neck. Then they took Schmidt to the hospital. Broder dropped me off at my car before following them. I drove home.

When I got back to the condo, Betty was upset.

"What happened to your neck?" she demanded.

"Wolfbitme" I mumbled, hoping she would drop the subject, but there was not much chance of that.

"What did you say?"

"It's nothing. There was a little accident in an alley after the Green Party meeting."

"You didn't get into a brawl with those guys, did you?"

"Not a physical one."

"Then what happened to your neck?"

"Look, there's nothing to worry about. Broder and Schmidt showed up. What could be safer than that?"

"Well, maybe you're right. Why were Broder and Schmidt there?"

"They wouldn't tell me, but I think they were following me."

"That's crazy. You are so paranoid. Why would they be following you?"

"Because they're investigating the shooting, of course."

"Ridiculous. Not everything is about you, you know."

"Well, that's a relief. Otherwise I might have taken it personally that I was attacked by a big honker animal in an alley tonight. That probably was a coincidence."

"Right," she agreed uncertainly.

"And since everything is not about me, I don't have to worry about this little bite on my neck turning me into a werewolf, do I?"

Silence. Then: "Would you make a martini for me, please?"

About an hour later, I slipped out of the condo and walked over to the large trash container next to the apartment building across the street. Opening the lid, I found the surveillance team. They appeared to be fully equipped for their work. Sherlock, a skinny guy with snarled hair, was aiming a telescope straight into my face from a distance of about six inches. "Wow, man," he said. "Your nose is really gross on the inside." His partner was Lew Archer, a very large black man who pretty much filled the dumpster. He was leaning back in a relaxed fashion on the trash behind him. The two of them were sitting on a blanket and had an empty pizza box opened in front of them. Both of them were smoking and a large sweet-smelling cloud surrounded the dumpster.

"Are you guys all set?" I asked.

"We're cool, man," they chorused.

"Do you know what you're watching for?"

"Howlers," Sherlock replied.

"Great," I said, then left quickly. If they got busted, I didn't want to be around when it happened.

Miracle of miracles, we heard no howling that night. The next morning, before dawn, I went out to see if my surveillance team had survived the night. They were loading their stuff into Lew's old car. Neither of them looked at me.

"How'd it go?" I asked them.

"Mission accomplished," Lew said.

"Really? What happened?"

"They found us here in the dumpster."

"Yeah?" Shivers were running up and down my spine.

"Yeah," Lew answered. "They wanna talk with you. Here. Tonight. Midnight."

"No problem." We were silent for a moment, thinking about the coming meeting. Then I added. "By the way, I really appreciate your doing this for me."

"No problem, man," Lew said. "But don't ask for nothin' like this again. It was too creepy for me."

The two finished stowing their blankets in the trunk and opened the front doors. As Sherlock was climbing in, he said to me. "Those dudes are weird, man. Way weirder than us." Then they drove away, black smoke belching out of their exhaust pipe.

CHAPTER 9. INTERVIEW WITH A WEREWOLF

The office was deserted when I arrived early the next morning. That suited me perfectly. I used the opportunity to go through the file cabinets, pulling out documents and reports. My goal was to try to find out more about the functioning of the branch office. How was the budget allocated, who controlled the accounts, were there any obviously missing pieces of expensive equipment, and so on. Did I expect to find that Brandi was cooking the books? No, I did not. Even though we did not like each other much, I could not say that Brandi appeared to be a dishonest person. Besides, not being an accountant, I would not be able to detect fraud even if it was right under my nose. And if Brandi was a crook, she was smart enough not to leave evidence out where I would be able to find it.

No, I was not looking for evidence of serious fraud, though a little fiddling around was not outside the realm of possibility. Mainly, I was nursing a vague hope that I could find out what Brandi was hiding from me. After all, her reluctance to give me an adequate understanding of the operations of the place might have just been due to her desire to maintain her unbridled power, or it might indicate that she was making decisions that would not withstand scrutiny.

Being a researcher in my first career, I started my snooping expedition with some hypotheses. Hypotheses are meant to be disproved; they just give you a starting point in an investigation. My hypotheses were as follows.

1. Brandi and Wilma were claiming extra work hours. Both were taking time off and covering for each other.
2. Brandi was ordering software, computer equipment and other office supplies for home use.
3. Brandi was charging inappropriate expenses to client accounts.
4. Brandi was offering special deals on insurance to friends.
5. Brandi was moonlighting on company time.
6. Brandi was accepting gifts from vendors in exchange for special treatment.
7. Brandi was charging expenses to the office that were not appropriate, such as mileage for her SUV.
8. Brandi was in cahoots with one or more of the reps on items one through seven above.

After an hour of searching through the files, I had to surrender. If any of my hypotheses were correct, I would never have been able to detect it on my own. As Clint Eastwood said in one of his movies, "A man has got to recognize his limitations." That was right before he blew away Hal Holbrook. Anyway, I just was not equipped to figure out what was really going on with the business.

When Brandi arrived, I followed her into her office.

"Good morning," I began.

"Good morning," was her guarded reply.

"There is something I need to talk to you about."

"Yes?" Her body language revealed nothing.

"Well. It's standard practice when a manager leaves to have a formal audit of the accounts, including a review of the inventory. In a small office like this, that should not be too much of a disruption."

"That is not standard practice. We have never done it here." Brandi was spitting the words at me.

"It's commonly done around the country. Do you want to arrange it or should I call Corporate?"

She glared at me, unsure of whether to defy me or to fake cooperation. She opted for defiant cooperation. "I'll call Corporate myself," she declared.

"When?"

"When I have time."

"What exactly are you doing this morning that would prevent you from calling Corporate?"

She dropped into her office chair, which, by the way, was a nice leather affair with several levers on the side for controlling angle, spring, and altitude. "I will try to reach someone about it today," she conceded. She looked tired.

I thanked her and went back to my office.

When the reps arrived at midday they immediately noted the chilly atmosphere. Jerry came to my office while Brandi and Wilma were at lunch and asked me what was going on. I told him I had requested an audit.

"Why?" he asked. "This place is run efficiently. We aren't losing money."

The papers on my desk were in disarray, so I tidied them up. Then I lined up my pens, stapler, tape dispenser and mouse in a neat row in front of me. He waited patiently. Finally, I said, "Due diligence."

"Due diligence? What's that?"

"Just making sure. CYA. Trying to do a responsible job."

"You're temporary here. Why do you care? Why don't you just relax, draw your pay, and enjoy a vacation?"

This irritated me. "Maybe I'm not built that way. If something turns out to be rotten later, I don't want anyone to be able to say that it was going on right under my nose."

"You smell a rat?"

"Something is odd about this place."

"Maybe it's just a power struggle with Brandi. Maybe you want her to be more subservient, the old male chauvinist pig thing."

DEAD MAN AT ANCHOR

"I thought about this audit before launching the idea. Exploring my own motivations was part of the process. Yes, this has elements of a power struggle. Bottom line, though, is that I am the one who is responsible here, even if it's only temporary. So, when she freezes me out, I have to up the ante."

"Even if it wrecks the operation?"

"If an audit wrecks the operation then something is rotten in this barrel of apples."

"You know, one of the other managers tried to have it out with Brandi. He's not around any more."

"Since I don't plan to stay around anyway, I can afford to risk pissing her off."

"You've got more guts than I do, Ed." With that remark, he went back to his office.

That afternoon, when I went down the street to the restaurant for a coffee and a cookie, guess which two people were sitting at a booth with their heads together, talking quietly and with great seriousness? You got it right the first time: Brandi and Jerry. I just smiled at them, and sat on the other side of the room so as to not disturb their conversation. Hypothesis number 8 was looking pretty strong at that point.

That evening Andrew and I met at Bienfang's again. He asked how things were going at the branch office. After I had updated him, he called me a trouble maker. I didn't mind; Andrew would have acted like a bulldog if he had been in my shoes. He would have dug into the investigation and not let up until he understood everything that was going on. He had investigation in his blood. He was not an unreasonable guy, though. Once he understood who was guilty of what, he could be lenient. But he didn't like to be fooled.

"Did it bother you to find out that Jerry was ratting you out to Brandi about your suspicions?"

"He didn't rat me out. He probably told her I smelled a rat, but she would have figured that out on her own. In fact," I went on, "I was counting on one of the reps running to Brandi with the news that I suspected dirty deeds were being committed. The goal here is to flush out any crooks. I'm shaking the tree."

"Do you think Brandi and Jerry are sleeping together?" Andrew wondered.

"Maybe, but I doubt it."

"Then why did he run to her? If she is possibly robbing the company, he shouldn't be trying to warn her. Are they ripping off the business together?"

"It's possible, but I would only give it a 50-50 chance."

"Then, why? Do you think he values personal loyalty more than honesty?"

"Come on, Andrew. That's pretty abstract. Most people don't think like that."

"Alright, you tell me. Why did Jerry run to Brandi to talk about the audit?"

"Because people like to talk, especially salesmen."

"You mean you were counting on at least one of the three reps being a gossipy weasel? That's pretty cynical."

"You have me figured wrong."

"Yeah?"

"Yep. I think one out of three would be a low estimate."

Andrew got a laugh out of that one.

We got on the subject of New Orleans, which was still reeling from the impact of Hurricanes Katrina and Rita. Months after the disaster, only half the population had moved back into the city. Congress planned to spend an enormous amount of money on rebuilding the place. I argued the 'con' position, while Andrew took 'pro'.

"All those people lost their homes and everything they owned due to no fault of their own. This is exactly the kind of situation where the government needs to help.

If a disaster hit up here, tax dollars would flow in from other parts of the country to help out." Andrew was giving it his best shot.

"In the Midwest, when somebody gets flooded out because he built his place in a flood plain, we don't rebuild his house for him, especially not in the same spot. So, why should we rebuild New Orleans? The whole place is in a flood plain."

"Don't you have any sympathy for those people? And what about the businesses that have been hurt? Don't you have any sympathy for the business owners?"

"Last I heard, carrying insurance was just good business practice and it was required for anybody with a mortgage. Insurance payouts should allow everybody to relocate somewhere else. For people who did not have insurance for their homes, let's give them a trailer somewhere above sea level."

"New Orleans is an important port. And rebuilding it would be good for the economy."

"If we need the port for national defense, we can rebuild that part of the place. But what you really are saying is that tax dollars should help out casinos and the oil industry. And if that wasn't bad enough, you're forgetting that the contracts for reconstruction will go to very large companies that are in bed with crooked politicians. If we rebuild New Orleans, it will be giant transfer of money from the average tax payer to big corporations, organized crime, and various fat cats. The whole idea falls down under scrutiny. This isn't about helping the poor people of New Orleans; that's just an excuse for a big corporate giveaway."

"You must be the most cynical guy in the state."

"But am I wrong?"

Back at the condo, Betty and I settled in to read for awhile before going to bed. Betty distracted me with a giggle.

"What's so funny?" I asked her.

"The cats are watching you."

They were indeed. Both of them were sitting in front of me, watching me intently.

"Cats are weird. It's not like I'm doing anything interesting. I'm just reading." The cats continued to watch me. I waved my arm at them. Their eyes swiveled in tandem, watching my hand.

"You know, I think they are worked up about this werewolf business," Betty announced. "They want you to make it stop, so we can get back to normal."

"Nah, they're just getting rambunctious. Bucky has been knocking dishes off the counter just to hear the crash. Yesterday the two of them had the food bowl on its side. They were flipping it up so that it would wobble around."

Betty laughed. "I saw that. And did you know they locked themselves in the bathroom the other day?"

"No kidding?"

"It was Saturday. When I came back from the store they were locked in the bathroom."

"Did you shut them in there after your shower?"

"They always go into the shower when I'm finished to lick the soapy water, but I most certainly did not lock them in. Bucky must have closed the door by banging on it. It's a good thing it happened on a weekend instead of on a work day."

"You're right about that. If they had been locked in your bathroom for ten hours, they would have destroyed it."

"Speaking of weekends, why don't you ever take me anywhere?"

"Eh?"

"You know what I'm talking about. We never go anywhere."

"You mean like staying up late, spending money, stuff like that?"

"See, you're being negative and I haven't even told you what I want to do."

"Okay, what do you want to do?"

"This weekend, up in Madison, there is a recital by a Dutch violinist. He is supposed to be very good."

"Okay, let's go."

Betty was shocked. "Just like that? I don't have to talk you into it?"

"No, sounds interesting."

"You've never been interested in recitals before."

"This is different. How often do you get to see a duck play a fiddle?"

"Duck? What duck?"

"You said you wanted to go see a duck violinist."

"*Dutch*, not *duck*, you idiot!"

"Well, that's not nearly as interesting."

That evening at midnight, I slipped out of bed without waking Betty. Bundling up in my warmest outdoor gear and taking a folding chair under my arm, I went outside, sat in a dark spot by the trash bin, and waited for contact. Naturally, I lighted up my pipe. "Ed," I told myself, "you have done some strange things in your time, but this has to take the cake. Sitting out in the dark cold waiting for a werewolf. Hmmff."

After I had loaded up the pipe for the second time, I realized that a shadowy figure was sitting on its haunches in the darkness just far enough away to be difficult to see.

When he realized that I was aware of him, he began our conversation with a comment: "Not everyone wants an apartment or even a trailer."

"Ah," I thought, "the two homeless guys at the library must be with this group."

My companion continued. "Some people want to live rough. That doesn't harm anyone."

"Fair enough, but what do you want from me?"

"We want that crowd of vigilantes to stop hunting us. We just want to be left alone."

"They think you killed the manager of the insurance office in Jefferson."

"We know they think that. It wasn't us." He chuckled. "Look, I can't tell you what killed that guy, but if it looked like animal bites, then it probably was animal bites. Sometimes a dog is just a dog, you know. You don't have to dream up werewolves to explain the situation. You've got some mass hysteria going on here. We want you to help chill them out."

"I see your point. Don't blame you a bit. I'll do what I can, but that may not be much." With our main business finished, I asked the fellow where his group had came from.

"Most of the Ruffers living around here started in remote areas of Canada. We gradually drifted south due to over-crowding. Ruffers need lots of roaming room. We like to hang out in woods watching people who are running around at night. When people start to notice and tell stories about us, we move on."

The Ruffer chuckled, deep in his throat. "I used to have a lot of fun watching people go out in the woods to cut firewood even during the day. When you don't watch television, you learn to enjoy simpler forms of entertainment, such as people-watching."

"How does a person get to be a Ruffer?"

"We pick up a few new recruits from among the homeless and hermits. Ruffers have always existed on the periphery of civilized society. When regular people see us, they just assume we are ordinary homeless guys. Most of us started out that way. But the true Ruffer has developed the ability to tolerate cold weather, run faster and farther than most people, hitch rides on the back ends of trucks, catch and eat wild animals raw. We rarely go indoors, never eat cooked food (unless it's in a garbage can), and never go to a hospital or see a doctor. We rarely congregate with each other. The only reason a few of us got together this time was because of those hunters; they were getting dangerous. We are non-violent, so we aren't going to fight them. But we aren't ready to vacate the region either, because there not many underdeveloped areas are left where we could be safe and unnoticed. Since you had come to our attention as being an unusually open-minded guy, we decided to approach you and ask for your help."

"Aren't you worried that I will tell the world about you? CNN might take camera crews out in the woods to look for you."

He laughed out lout. "Nobody would believe this story, so we're not worried about getting discovered."

"What do you guys do when you get old? Living rough must become a little more difficult when you get arthritis or whatever."

My companion chuckled again. "We move to Florida like everybody else."

"What?" I was amazed.

"Just joshing you. We don't buy condos, of course. Look, many of us eventually die in the woods or are found in a field. Some of the older ones migrate south for warmer weather and might even end up living on a beach. I'll do that myself someday, if I last long enough. At this stage in my life, though, hot weather is no fun at all. Once you get acclimated to living outdoors during the winter in the far North, summers in the deep south are intolerable."

"Makes sense to me," I responded. All in all, it was a friendly and educational conversation. But the cold was seeping into my bones, so I needed to wrap things up.

"If you don't mind, I have two more questions for you," I said. "First, do Ruffers ever drop out, dropping back into regular society.?"

"Oh., now and then one of us gets lazy, hangs around a farm for the scraps he can pull out of the garbage. But, look, that is not the same as doing what you call a return to regular society. Society is not going to accept one of us. Once you have learned to live the way we do, people are uncomfortable around us."

"An unusual person might accept you. After all, I'm sitting here talking to you, aren't I?"

"Well, occasionally some kind of liaison between a Ruffer and another person might develop." This was a reluctant admission, but it changed to a humorous tone. "After all, there's no accounting for love."

The idea of love between a dirty Ruffer and 'regular person' was so odd it made me chuckle. "Okay," I went on, "second question. You said you guys are non-violent. How can you be sure that all of you are non-violent? Any group has variation from one individual to the next. Could one Ruffer be a murderer?"

My companion was silent while he mulled that over. "That is an interesting question. A renegade Ruffer? Yes, I suppose it's possible. Under normal circumstances, it would never happen. But if a Ruffer became intimately involved with people, by falling in love, for example, then anything could happen. After all, every evil under the sun is perpetrated by people. That is one of the reasons Ruffers become Ruffers: to escape human evil."

By this time I was thoroughly chilled, so I thanked my companion, promised to do what little I could about his request, and turned to go back inside. But before I went, I had to throw out one last question: "What's with the howling?" But my nameless friend was gone, leaving a throaty chuckle in the air.

CHAPTER 10. INTERVIEW WITH A WEREWOLF HUNTER

The next morning I took a day off from work and drove over to the convenience store outside Whitewater where I had first heard of the werewolf hunters. The young man whom I had spoken with before was on duty. He agreed to pass along my request to meet with someone from the group. After that, I went to Wal-Mart to pick up some underwear. When I got back to my car, an old pickup truck was idling next to it. The rack in the back window held two rifles. A couple of hefty guys in floppy-eared hats were sitting in the front seat, staring at me.

The one in the driver's seat rolled down his window, spat into the snow at my feet, and said, "Get in." I climbed in on the passenger side, sitting pressed against the door. The other passenger handed me a stocking cap, and told me to put it on and pull it all the way down over my face. I did so, and then the truck started moving. About ten minutes later, we were bouncing along a rutted road. Shortly after that, we stopped, and the hat was pulled from my head.

We had arrived at a hunting lodge. Trees were all around it. No other habitation was visible. We appeared to be far removed from any potential witnesses to what was about to transpire. This fact did not reassure me that I would be treated well.

They led me inside. We kicked the snow off of our boots, hung our coats on hooks by the door then went into a large room where several silent men sat at a picnic table, cleaning their rifles. The fireplace contained several large logs that were heating the room nicely.

The two men who had brought me sat down in chairs at the back of the room, leaving me standing in front of the fireplace. A large man with a shock of white hair peered down the barrel of his rifle to assure himself that it was clean then closed the breech. He looked up at me and frowned then gestured with his head toward a vacant spot at the picnic table. "Sit," he said. I sat.

"Heard you wanted to talk," he said.

"You must be the fellahs that are out to shoot the, uh, wild dogs that are in the area."

"Wild dogs. Huh." He glared at me. "What if we are?"

"Somebody could get hurt." Both of us were thinking about the dead man who was found at the antique mall. Mentioning a murder seemed unnecessarily direct at that moment, so I let the thought pass unvoiced.

The old man was powerfully built. He was wearing a red flannel shirt. Wide suspenders held up his dungarees. His green boots were rubberized and had dried mud on the tread, which I could see when he stretched out his legs and crossed them at the ankles.

"You got that right," he said. "Shooting something generally hurts it. Whether we are talking about somebody or something is a different question. Why should you care if we kill some wild dogs? Or even a wolf?"

Here was my moment. I swallowed hard. "A fellah spoke to me last night. He said you killed a...colleague of his. He said it was a mistake. His crowd hasn't hurt anyone. They want to be left alone. He asked me to deliver the message."

The old man glared me. "You're delivering messages for a pretty strange bunch, mister."

"They're strange, but they did me no harm."

"Do you believe this story, that they don't hurt people?"

64

"I believe most of them don't. Any barrel can have a bad apple, though."

The old hunter nodded. "You got that right. And sometimes the whole barrel goes bad, rotten, unholy bad."

"You can't be sure that is true in this situation."

"What about that dead insurance man in Jefferson?"

"The one I spoke to said they didn't do it."

"What about the pets that have been killed around here?"

"He didn't mention that. Maybe I could ask him if he can put a stop to it."

He leaned toward me. "Listen, mister. I don't know who you are. But you don't know what you're dealing with here. Those things don't die unless they are shot in the heart with a silver bullet. I can tell you that for free."

"Maybe so. But that doesn't mean they killed anyone. It just means you killed someone."

He gave me an angry look. "Tell you what. If the cops catch the one that killed the insurance man, then we'll hold off on shooting silver bullets. At least for now. But if they don't catch somebody in a couple of days, or if somebody else dies, then it's war. We ain't waiting around till it's too late."

It wasn't much, but it was the best I could get out of him.

As they drove me back to the Wal-Mart, my eyes covered again, I had to ask myself why I was involved in that mess. "Sure," I thought. "Some weird guy in the dark asks me to talk to some crazy werewolf hunter. Okay, a hitchhiker I didn't even know was murdered. That's not my concern." I continued on in this vein for awhile, but it was just nerves. It was too late to complain. I was involved and, as far as I could tell, the only way to get out of the impending cross-fire was to help the police catch the real killer. But, could they catch him? And if they did, would it be a human being, or a wolf?

CHAPTER 11. GRANNY, WHAT SHARP TEETH YOU HAVE!

Heavy wet snow was falling during the drive to Jefferson the next morning. When I parked in the lot behind the building it was only seven, but Brandi's SUV was already in its place. I had left the warm confines of my car and was reaching for the handle of the office door when I heard a distant shout. Looking around, I could just barely see Brandi through the pre-dawn light down the street, by the railroad tracks near the river. She was waving at me, so I obligingly trudged through the new-fallen snow toward her. The snow was wet. "This stuff will melt fast," I said to myself. "Spring is just around the corner, and boy am I ready for it!"

That happy thought was filling my mind and putting a smile on face when I reached the corner where Brandi was standing. "Good morning," I offered. That's me, always trying to be polite, when I can remember to do so, which is only about half the time.

Brandi gave me her flat stare for an uncomfortable few seconds. Then she broke into a big smile. It was infectious, so I smiled back at her. We were grinning at each other like a couple of giddy teenagers.

"You just wouldn't stop, would you?" she asked me with that broad smile.

My smile faltered a bit. "What do you mean?" I asked her guardedly.

"You know what I mean. Poking around, sticking your nose in where it didn't belong. You couldn't just leave well enough alone."

"Just doing my job."

"It wasn't your job. Your job was to sit in that chair and leave me alone. I know how to run this office. I've been doing it for years. I didn't need any help from you. And I sure didn't need you to stir up trouble."

"I'm sorry you feel that way. Managers are supposed be accountable for what they do. Everything we do should stand up under scrutiny from Corporate."

"Corporate doesn't give a damn what we do as long as we don't cause trouble. Look, I'm done arguing with you. You're terminated."

"You can't terminate me, Brandi. You must be out of your mind."

"Oh, I can terminate you alright." She stepped around the corner of the building for a second then returned pulling a heavy chain behind her. At the end of the chain was a very large dog. He let his mouth hang open as he breathed, saliva dripping from his fangs. The monster looked as if he remembered me. The expression on his face seemed to say, "You got away last time, but this time I'll make a meal out of you."

"That's a very impressive animal," I said. "What kind is he?"

"I don't know. He just wandered up to my house one day. He's very intelligent. I didn't need to train him to attack my enemies. He does that out of love. And you certainly fit the definition of an enemy." She dropped to one knee, unhooked his chain, pointed at me, and shouted shrilly: "Kill, Wolf! Kill!"

Fear makes flat feet fleet. I knew the animal could outrun me in a second, so I ran straight across the railroad tracks out into the river. Running into a river in the middle of the winter season in Wisconsin may not seem like a wise decision, and maybe it wasn't, but in my defense, just let me say my options were limited.

The water was shallow near the street, but dropped off quickly. It came up to my thighs almost immediately. Chunks of ice floated by my face when the weight I dreaded struck me in the center of the back and drove me under the surface. The freezing temperature made my heart stop in my chest. "Don't drink this stuff," I thought inanely. "It's polluted." The weight on my back drove me down to the bottom, arms outstretched. My hand closed around a brick that was lying near it. Up I came, dragging in a great gasp of air. Wolf latched onto my left arm with his powerful jaws, trying to pull me back under the surface. Instinctively, I swung the brick in an overhead arc with all of my strength, bringing it down directly on his matted head. The brick bounced off his skull and flew from my hand back into the water.

Wolf paused his murderous assault. His eyes rolled slightly then he released his grip on my arm, heading for the river wall that separated us from the street. I followed him. Together we crawled out of the water and collapsed on the railroad tracks, dripping and gasping. Ice was forming in my hair and my face felt numb. My bare hands were grasping the steel tracks, but I could not feel the cold metal. I managed to drag myself upward onto my hands and knees. Turning, Wolf and I locked stares; he blinked, whimpered and ran away, his feet slipping and scrabbling for traction as he disappeared from sight.

Footsteps came up to me. I could see the leather boots Brandi was wearing. "You hurt Wolf," she hissed, the she swung her leg over my back, straddled me, and tightly wrapped Wolf's chain around my neck. The pain was excruciating, but I was too tired to resist. I just crouched there, on all fours, waiting for her to finish me off.

"Stop! Police!" My ears heard the shout before its meaning registered on my mind.

"Step away from that man! Step away or I'll shoot!"

Brandi's weight lifted from my back and the chain came loose from my neck, dropping with a protracted clunk onto the pavement. Turning my head, I was able to see Sergeant Schmidt about twenty feet away, aiming her service revolver at Brandi. One of Schmidt's arms was heavily bandaged.

"Don't move!" Schmidt said.

Broder appeared at my side and helped me to my feet.

"Don't move," Schmidt repeated to Brandi. "Look, I'm putting the gun away." She wore her holster under her trench coat on the hip opposite from her gun hand. Opening the coat, she inserted the gun and let the coat drop closed. Then, she held up her hands in a placating gesture.

Brandi held her hands up also. But instead of gesturing for calm, her body language sent a different signal. Her legs assumed a wide stance. Her hands were held out at her sides. Her eyes narrowed to slits.

"Watch out!" I yelled, but it was too late.

Brandi dropped to one knee. Her coat and skirt slid up over her muscular leg to reveal a holster strapped onto her nylon-encased thigh. She pulled it out and pointed it in a two-handed grip toward Schmidt with one smooth motion.

Brandi got off the first shot as Schmidt reached to draw her own weapon. The sharp crack of Brandi's gun was followed by three quick retorts from Schmidt's. There was a moment of silence then Brandi dropped over onto the cement, facing upward. Three holes in her forehead formed the corners of a perfect triangle.

Schmidt walked up to Broder and me as we gazed down into Brandi's tranquil face. "Thanks," I said to her. "You saved my life."

She gave me her best glare. "Now we're even. But don't get the wrong idea. I still hate your guts." Then she turned away to call for the meat wagon.

I looked at Broder and he looked at me, then he shook his head and laughed. "That's my partner," he said. "Isn't she something?"

"You can say that again."

WHAT SHARP TEETH YOU HAVE!

"Does she hate everybody as much as she hates me?"
"No. Just you."
"Thanks. That makes me feel really special."

CHAPTER 12. CONCLUSION

The afternoon temperature was a balmy 34 degrees Fahrenheit. The sunny, spring-like day lifted everyone's spirits. What made it even better was that it was a Saturday. All seemed right with the world. It was time to take a good long walk, to get the winter sloth out of my system.

From our condo, it only takes 30 minutes to walk over to McDonalds. I left home at about eight o'clock in the morning. If I wanted to, I could have walked past the big new recreational area down by the river, then walked along the river toward town. Crossing at the bridge, I could then swing past the newspaper offices, cross back over the river on the Main Street bridge, then meet Betty for breakfast at McDonalds. However, since I was not a nature lover, I would walk through the residential neighborhoods instead. Mother Nature was okay, but, frankly, she set off my allergies.

Betty ordinarily would not want to get out of bed so early on a weekend, but I had promised to drive her to the thrift store in Jefferson after we ate. She was up for that. Betty regarded purchases in a thrift store as donations to charity. That point of view allowed her to feel good about recreational shopping, which otherwise would run against her frugal upbringing. Betty usually found a way to make an end round around her frugal instincts, though being married to a tightwad had made it much more difficult for her.

CONCLUSION

The walk felt great. I arrived at McDonalds with my blood singing in my veins, my nose red from the brisk air, and a smile on my face.

And I had other reasons to smile. For one thing, I would not have to go back to the insurance office in Jefferson; that job was finished. The shootout in Jefferson had been two weeks previous, so the policy inquiry was over. In addition, the audit of the books by Corporate also was over. Now I could finally put all that behind me. Corporate had asked me to take on another temporary assignment, but I refused. That job in Jefferson had not been fun, except, of course, the mystery itself. Finding out who killed the previous manager was a thrill. And finding out about the story behind the dead man at the anchor store also had been lots of fun. Corporate did not accept my refusal of their offer lightly, unfortunately. They said they would give the matter some thought and come up with something I might like better.

Betty and I had breakfast then drove up to Jefferson. The thrift store was having a half-price sale, so it was clear that Betty would be tied up for a while. To pass the time, I went over to the discount hair-cutting place and had a trim. Cutting my own hair, as I usually do, makes it a bit ragged. A touch-up now and then can be helpful.

While sitting in the barber's chair, the woman cutting my hair asked me what I had been up to lately. I told I had been solving murders and talking to werewolves. She did not appear to believe me, which is a disappointment. However, I had long before gotten used to people not believing everything I told them. Heck, if I intended to lie to them I would have made a more believable story. Even so, most people had to get to know me before they realized that while I might be eccentric, I sometimes knew what I was talking about. The challenge for them was to figure out which times I was right and which times I was out to lunch.

Andrew, Emily, Betty and I met at four at Sal's that evening for a long-planned review of the murder cases. Sal's was one of our favorite places to eat or just have a beer. Sal's had a nice restaurant on one side and a large bar on the other. It was close to where all of us lived and was the perfect place to review recent events.

During the previous week, the police had filled me in on all the known facts of the case as it related to Brandi and the insurance office. I reported all this to the group. Understandably, they had a few questions.

"Why did Brandi do it?" Emily asked. "And am I right in assuming her dog killed the previous bank manager, as well as being directed to attack you?"

"How can we know for sure what her motivations were? I guess she was unbalanced. She displayed a lot of repressed anger. It appeared to me that she was one of those people who always insist on having their own way. Unfortunately, the weak leadership at the branch office allowed her to have her own way all the time. She became used to it. Then, when she was threatened by potential loss of control, she saw murder as self-defense."

Betty had a different theory. "I bet she was divorced. I bet she was abused by some man and then dumped. She had to fend for herself in the world, so she had to be tough, to become a survivor."

Andrew changed the subject, thank goodness. "Was Jerry involved?" he asked.

"No. He was just a gossip who got the occasional favor from her. Mainly, he liked the weak supervision of the office because it was less restrictive. Can't blame him for that."

Andrew was not quite satisfied. "Was Brandi ripping the place off?"

"Apparently there was no major fraud going on. Sure, Brandi and Wanda took lots of time off and covered for each other. Wanda had almost nothing she was required to do. No, Brandi did not commit murder to cover up some

CONCLUSION

giant rip-off she had perpetrated. Her motivation must have been a desire to maintain control."

"Well, that fits," Betty said.

We all looked at her. "What do you mean?" Emily asked.

"All crime is motivated by money, power or love. Brandi's desire for control is the same as a desire for power. It fits."

It did fit. And, I thought to myself, it also explained why Wolf committed murder for her. He was not after power or money, so it had to be love.

"Change of subject, you guys," I announced, pulling a folded piece of paper out of my pocket. "I came up with an idea for a change in government policy and I want your opinions on which political party might be willing to adopt it."

My audience groaned. "You have too much time on your hands," Betty said.

I started reading anyway. "Whereas affordable transportation is an important requirement for obtaining a job, and

"Whereas, traveling at high speeds increases the risk of injury, and

"Whereas, increasing fuel efficiency is essential for reducing national dependence on fossil fuels,

"Be it resolved that vehicles weighing less that 1500 pounds *and* having fuel efficiency greater than 50 miles per gallon *and* having a purchase price of less than $5000 *and* having a top speed of less than 50 miles per hour shall be exempt from all licensing and inspection regulations and fees."

My audience met this proposal with flat stares and dead silence. Finally, Andrew said, "No political party will endorse that."

He was right, of course. I wadded up the proposal and stuffed it back into my pocket. I still think it was a darn   good   idea.

CHAPTER 13. EPILOGUE

After dinner, we went back to our condo. As I was smoking my pipe, I mused about my plans for the coming week. I had none, which causing me some discomfort, though I tried to be upbeat about it. Betty had tried to teach me that time off is not something you have to endure between activities. Even so, time off generally caused me to become bored after a couple of hours.

Betty opened the door into the garage and handed me my cell phone. "It's somebody from the insurance company," she announced. I sighed; they were still after me. They were pleased with the results of my temporary assignment, not because it turned out so well, but because it cleaned up a mess that was bound to cause problems sooner or later.

Corporate had promised me a nice bonus when they asked me to take on another assignment as a temporary manager, but I had firmly declined because day-to-day management was just too boring for me. If I had been any good as a manager, I would have spent my time managing instead of investigating werewolves. Corporate was disappointed, but they said they were not going to give up on me.

This time, it was my friend Steve Winters on the phone. He was the fellow who ran the Fort Atkinson branch office and who had recommended me for the temporary position in Jefferson. He reported that Corporate had asked him to sell me on the idea of working as a company investigator. They wanted me to be a freelancer working on contract to their internal security division.

"Okay, Steve, I'll do it," I said. "But I will only take on occasional jobs, and then I will only do it if they team me with an experienced investigator. I won't stay overnight away from home more than two nights in a row. And, I don't want to stay up late on stake-out because I fall asleep at ten. And I flatly refuse to drive in Chicago."

"You don't have to worry about any of that, Ed."

"Well, then, what was it you guys were expecting me to do?"

"Just be yourself, Ed, just be yourself."

"What does that mean?"

"It means that if we put you into an office where we know something dirty is going down, pretty soon things will start to happen. The stuff will hit the fan. You will just go around prying into things and tripping over yourself and next thing you know, the case will be solved."

"Thank you, I think. You are showing a lot of confidence in my abilities."

"Yes, your abilities are tremendous. But what will make you outstandingly effective as an internal investigator are your flaws. You are a neurotic, obsessive, compulsive, irritating, persistent, paranoid, judgmental, over-imaginative, flakey, bull-in-a-china-shop. That makes you the perfect guy for internal investigations. Without even trying, you become a catalyst, a lightning rod, causing all the dishonest crap around to reach melt-down temperature. Other companies will be envious that we have a hot-shot guy like you, which is why we are going to keep it a big secret."

"Gee, I don't know what to say."

"You should say 'thanks, I'll take the job.'" Steve had something more to add to his pitch. "Do you know what your problem is, Ed?"

"No, you better tell me."

"You lack self-confidence. That's why you feel guilty unless you are working your tail off. You shouldn't feel guilty. You will get the job done even if you goof off most of the day. Just lighten up."

With a pep talk like that, how could I turn him down? Besides, this job was certain to lead to a number of interesting situations. I suspected I was going to enjoy my new gig.

Over the weeks that followed, life in Fort Atkinson and the surrounding region settled back down, though not everything was quite the same as it had been before the murder of the insurance man. Now that the murderer had been caught, the 'Ruffers' were quietly co-existing with the regular people in the area. Pets no longer disappeared. An injured hunter was helped by a strange guy who would not speak to him and who disappeared before he could be thanked. A motorist who slid off the road late at night was carried into town and left in the Wal-Mart. A drug addict who robbed a convenience store was attacked by a dog. The vigilante group disbanded. Local people still told the werewolf myth, but the werewolves were reported to be protectors, not threats.

Every now and then, my nameless friend would join me for a chat by the dumpster at midnight. He was an interesting character. We discussed politics, society, religion, and crime. During one of those chats I intended to ask him if he could explain why a middle-aged guy like me would suddenly start growing hair over his previously hairless body. I was sure it was just normal aging and only an over-active imagination would suggest otherwise. But why was my vision better and my hearing more acute? Why was I asking for rare steak instead of medium-well? And why was I feeling more aggressive?

I never got around to asking those questions, because I gradually realized that Betty was enjoying the new me. It must be true what they say: women tend to like a guy who is a bit of a beast. And to top it off, Bucky and I became

77

fast friends. We became a dynamic duo: Bad Boy Bucky and Wild Man Ed, the Terrors of the Condo.

DEAD MAN ALOFT

This book is dedicated to all those good Christians
who mentally cross their fingers every time they recite the
creed on Sunday morning.

PART ONE

CHAPTER 1. WHAT FALLS FROM THE SKY?

The little airplane had its steps set up and waiting for the small group of passengers. The commuter flight from Madison to Milwaukee was just the right size for the short hop, since it only had one line of seats on each side of the narrow aisle. The stewardess was tidying up the cabin, readying it for the next group. This was the last flight of the day and she was eagerly anticipating the return to her home base.

Most of the passengers were women dressed in business suits. As they climbed the narrow steps, they clutched their briefcases and purses tightly as the brisk wind fluttered their clothing and their hair. One by one they entered the cabin and selected their seats. None had overnight bags, suggesting that they were just returning from the capital after a one-day meeting. Briefcases went into the tiny overhead compartment and purses were placed on top of shiny shoes, feet held close together in the narrow space under the seat immediately in front of each passenger.

One passenger was strangely out of place. He was wearing a worn field jacket, baggy jeans, and a pair of dingy sneakers. His eyes displayed anxiety, flashing nervously from side to side behind his long unkempt hair. The man had a skinny neck, but his zippered coat was closed over a protruding belly. His bushy beard completed the ensemble.

The scruffy man took a seat in the back of the airplane then stared fixedly out of the window. Instead of watching the other passengers as they came aboard, he ignored them all, seemingly trying to fade into invisibility.

One of the last to board was a woman of stern demeanor and impeccable appearance. She was dressed in the latest business attire, purchased from the best stores. Her shoes alone cost more than most of the other female passengers spent on their entire wardrobes.

This passenger clearly was a senior executive in a major corporation. Every hair was in place and not a wrinkle was in sight. She carried herself with an air of authority that unconsciously was respected by those around her. Lesser mortals tended to give her the right of way when walking through doorways or down sidewalks. She accepted this degree of deference as her due.

The passenger with the expensive shoes was accompanied by a young man, also in a business suit. He sat across the aisle from her. Every aspect of his appearance revealed that he was intensely aware of her. If she wanted a document, he would produce it. If she needed to speak to someone on the phone, he would punch in the numbers and get the other party on the line. If she wanted a tissue, it would appear instantly in his outstretched hand.

When everyone was seated, the stewardess closed the door and made her usual announcements. The plane taxied toward the runway, hesitated, then rushed into the air. As is usual after takeoff, a general sense of relaxed tension spread through the cabin the air when the plane reached its cruising altitude.

The relaxation did not endure long. About ten minutes after departure, the raggedy man stood up and walked to the back of the cabin. Turning to face forward, he pulled a black water pistol from his side pocket. Only the stewardess saw him, since she was facing backward while the passengers all faced forward. She gasped at the sight of the pistol.

The man spoke out in a loud nervous voice. "Ladies," he said, ignoring the young man who so clearly was a lackey. "Look at me, please!" He held the pistol pointing upward.

Heads turned, mouths gasped, voices whimpered.

"Relax!" he said. "This is only a water pistol." He paused a moment, then went on. "But don't relax too much. It's full of indelible black ink. If I shoot you with it, your nice clothes will be ruined." He waved the pistol for effect. "Think about it. I will start squirting ink all around this plane if anybody gets in my way!"

"What do you want?" The question was asked by the woman with the expensive shoes. She did not appear to be frightened, only cautious and calculating.

"Don't worry; I ain't gonna take this plane to another country and I ain't gonna crash it." He looked around reassuringly. "I'm just gonna take your purses and jump out." Now that the action he had been planning was underway, he seemed less anxious and more in command of both himself and the situation. His bearing had become almost military in its air of calm competence.

He could see the women doing the calculations in their minds. Was the cash in their purses worth more than the suits on their bodies? All of them decided they would take the safe route of passivity. They did not want their clothes to be ruined. More importantly, they did not want to be knocked around by a man who, though he looked calm at the moment, clearly must not be entirely normal. After all, only a deranged person would hijack an airplane with a water pistol filled with ink. On the other hand, it appeared to be working, so perhaps the gentleman was not as crazy as he appeared at first glance.

The man, who might or might not have been insane, was very selective and very fast. He quickly took each purse that had a long strap. In turn each was slung over his head and shoulder. He was able to get five purses on one side and five on the other. When he came to the woman who had asked him what he wanted, she resisted giving him her leather satchel.

"It's not a purse, it's a briefcase," she said. "It only has papers in it."

"Yeah, right, lady," he growled, and jerked it out of her arms.

The young man who was the lackey to the woman with the expensive shoes started to rise to her defense, but she stayed him with glance.

"No, Arnie. Stop" she said, as to a dog. Arnie sat back down in his seat, clearly relieved that he was not called upon to be a heroic man of action.

Fully loaded, the bandit ordered the stewardess to open the door while he unzipped his jacket, revealing a parachute. She pulled levers and then strained against the door. When it swung open, three things happened almost at once. The wind blew fiercely through the cabin. The pilot began shouting questions over the speaker. And, of course, the scruffy man leaped out of the plane.

The thief entered the darkening sky over rural Jefferson County only ten minutes after the plane had taken off from the airport in Madison. He took with him miscellaneous valuables and cash, and also some highly secret and damaging documents. He was never seen again. The same could not be said of the documents.

The scruffy man dropped head first toward the earth. When he pulled the release, the parachute unfurled behind and above him. When it inflated, his downward plunge was suddenly arrested. He reached upward and grasped the control lines of his chute, but the jerk caused some of the bags to slip off of his shoulders. The heaviest bags slid down onto to his lift wrist, breaking his grip on the cords.

They flew out into the night. He snatched at them desperately, but they were gone, landing one by one with small plops in an arc that spread across a highway, a field of brush, and a street, with the last one landing square onto the deck of my second floor condo in Fort Atkinson, Wisconsin. When I went out the next morning to set up the stepladder so that I could replace the burned out bulb in the porch light, the leather satchel, now somewhat scuffed, was beside my wicker chair.

I loved a mystery, as most of us do. Here was an unexpected present for me. A briefcase from nowhere was deposited on my own porch. I had every right to investigate its contents. It practically begged me to open it. So, of course, I did. What choice did I have, really? And, of course, that is what got me into trouble, trouble that included corporate crime, political dirty tricks, and murder.

CHAPTER 2. ED WHO?

A couple of years before the airplane incident just described, Betty and I were university professors living in Texas. It was time to slow down a bit and to reconnect with our Midwestern roots, so we bought a second-floor condo in a new building in Fort Atkinson, Wisconsin, which is south-east of Madison and south-west of Milwaukee.

We did not realize when we bought the place that it would soon become our full-time home. That first summer turned out not to be restful. Though we very much enjoyed our small-town life, events conspired to interrupt our vacation. A body was found on the downstairs patio, right below our deck. This was the unit later purchased by our friend and neighbor Emily Eberhardt. The police suspected me of being involved in the murder. Naturally, I was pulled into the investigation, mainly to save my own skin.

That was how we got to know detective sergeants Broder and Schmidt, who you will read more about later. We also got to know our adopted home very well, and grew to like it very much. A couple of Betty's cousins lived in Fort (as the locals sometimes called it), which was nice for us. Everything we needed was either in walking distance or only required a short drive. We were close enough to Madison to be able to get the big city flavor when we needed it, but we rarely availed ourselves of that dubious benefit. And as for Milwaukee, we only went there when it was time to make an obligatory visit to the annual state fair.

Our summer home became a permanent home because of the murder investigation I just mentioned. By the time it was over, I had two strokes of good luck and two strokes of bad luck. The first stroke of good luck was that the case was solved without me having to go jail. The first bit of bad luck was that I had a heart attack at the end of it. The second bit of bad luck was that most of the events in the case were not only both outlandish and also only observed by me, so everyone decided I was nuts. The second bit of good luck was ending up with an extra hundred thousand dollars that was unaccounted for, having been slipped into my bank account in an attempt to discredit me and left there by a government investigator who felt guilty about the smear on my reputation.

We returned briefly to our jobs in Texas, but Betty decided that my weakened mental and physical health necessitated early retirement, not that I could ever completely retire. That would be too boring.

After moving all of our household things into the condo, we settled down into small town life. My wife, Betty, and I lived with our two cats, Fritter and Bucky. Betty, who was a physician, started working in a nearby clinic. I tried selling electric bicycle motors on the Internet. That did not work out very well, unless you can count the benefits of learning how not to succeed in business. After that, I worked as a consulting ethicist for a while, then took a job as an interim manager in an insurance office. Along the way, I picked up a part-time position as director of a charitable foundation that provided assistance to persons with serious and persistent mental illness. That was the job I enjoyed the most.

At the time the leather satchel fell onto my deck, I was about to undertake a new assignment; undercover work at a construction site where some items were being stolen on a regular basis. My friend Steve Winters was a manager for the insurance company that was using me as a free-lance investigator after my brief period as an interim manager. I was not a very good manager, but the insurance company thought I had a natural talent for flushing out criminal behavior. Since they were on the hook for the losses at the construction site, they called me in on the case.

That pretty much sums up the background you need to follow this story. That, unfortunately, does not mean you will understand everything that happened. How could you? I never did. I was just a silver-haired guy, five-feet, nine inches tall, 170 pounds, and regarded by all as somewhat eccentric. I was not a stupid guy, but this case involved shadowy forces that were far beyond anything ordinary people could fathom.

CHAPTER 3. ED GOES UNDERCOVER

I looked over the documents, but did not have time to make sense out of them that first evening. As far as I could tell, they consisted of correspondence between various food industry corporations about a coordinated lobbying strategy. That did not sound like it was entirely kosher, so I set the case aside for more careful analysis.

The next morning I rolled out of bed with some trepidation, though my anxiety had nothing to do with the documents. This was to be my first day undercover. The insurance company I free-lanced for was getting claims from a construction site located between my home and Jefferson, a town just a few miles up the road, so it was only natural that they would ask me to check it out. However, they probably did not realize that as a natural born geek, I was not likely to fit in well on a construction site. They assured me nothing could go wrong if I was assigned to drive a lift truck, one of the small ones. That sound like fun, sort of like driving a golf cart, so I agreed. They took me off for a little training in the operation of the vehicle then let me choose a false name to use on the construction site. My job was to find out who was steeling all the snack food.

The bright June sun was lighting up the parking lot when I arrived at the site. In Wisconsin, the winters are long so we always appreciate a nice day. Of course, when the temperature and the humidity rise during July and August, we start to miss the snow and ice. This particular day was perfect, but it was warm enough to give me an inkling of how sticky I would feel in another month.

The construction job was a 'big box' retail establishment that had been blocked for years by local activists. Finally, they lost a series of legal challenges, and the store was going up rapidly. The shell was finished and products were going into the warehouse on the back side of the building while the retail side was still in progress.

The big chain had a sophisticated computer system for keeping track of inventory. Somehow, they knew right away that some of the stock was disappearing. Most of the items stolen were low cost junk food, but tens of cases were disappearing each week. I supposed that when the building was done, cameras would watch every part of the store and theft would be more difficult. For now, however, all they could say was that more stock had been delivered than was actually present.

When I arrived that day, I parked my little Ford Focus next to about twenty large pickup trucks. The row of vehicles looked like a crew of cowboys had left their horses tied to the rail in front of a saloon, with one of them riding a burro.

A man with a harried look and a clipboard was walking around the store, so I chased him down and gave him my false name.

"Ed Shoemaker," I said. I had picked that name so it would be easy to remember.

"Shoemaker, yeah, right. They said you were due to start today." He looked me over without much enthusiasm. Since I was an over-fifty silver haired guy who only reached five-nine when wearing my boots, I could see why he was not impressed by my potential as a construction worker. "Here's your time card. Punch in over there, by the portajohn. Then grab a lift and pick up those cases of floor tiles and take them over to where the guys are putting down the flooring."

After climbing onto the lift, I trundled it over to the stacks of floor tiles. Carefully sliding the lifters into the gap in the first pallet, I hoisted it then gently ran it over to the construction team. By the time I got there, four hefty guys were watching me. Easing my load down in front of them, I called out, "Here ya go, guys."

The biggest of the four tilers did not exactly give me a pat on the head. "Do ya think you could go any slower there, Buddy?" he demanded.

This shook me up. I thought I was doing fine. "I'll speed it up," I replied.

"Yeah, why doncha. We ain't got all day here."

So, off we went, me and my little vehicle. This time I managed to load it up a little faster. And I drove it faster back over to where they putting in the floor. Even so, they still were all standing and watching me when I arrived. Those guys were pretty fast considering that bending over with such big guts must have been a challenge.

That was how my day went. I worked as quickly as I could, but the tillers were always waiting for me. The big guy, whose name was Bud Miller, usually had some kind of critical remark to make. He must have thought he was being clever. His buddies must have thought so too, because they always chuckled at his jokes.

By quitting time I was pretty disgusted. When I got home I sat on the deck and smoked my pipe for a while. You may think this is odd, but for several weeks I had been preoccupied with theology, so I returned to a running dialogue I had been having with myself. Before you get completely disgusted with me, let me reassure you that this does actually have something to do with the case.

The issue in my mind was identification of the essence or critical elements of Christianity. I had been raised a Protestant and still was one. But I had a difficult time accepting most of the elements of the creed we recited every Sunday morning and I was convinced most people in the congregation did not buy it either. Did that make us hypocrites? Were we non-Christians who did not belong in church at all? I did not think so. I thought the pastors were wrong and the congregations were right to question the creed while still considering themselves to be Christians. After all, we have a right, a *responsibility*, to make up our own minds on religious matters.

Here is what I figured most Christians actually believed, and it is quite a bit different from what the churches tell them they are supposed to believe. First, the Kingdom of Heaven is spiritual, not physical. It is accessible here and now by spiritual people. If there is an afterlife, it does not involve the physical bodies we carry around with us in this life.

Second belief: the bible contains stories that tell us what to believe and how to live. However, the historical accuracy of the bible is irrelevant and dubious. Parables are not true stories, but they still contain truths. Bible stories also contain truths, but may not be accurate from an historical point of view. This means many elements of the creed, from the statement 'born of the virgin Mary' onward, are unimportant.

Third belief: we are Christians because we believe Jesus Christ offers us an ability to understand how we can be spiritual, how we should relate to God, and how we should address moral issues. He is the human face of God. What was said and done 2000 years ago is not as important as what he does for each of us now. The Apostle Paul disagreed strongly with this position and he was a smart guy, but most people in their hearts don't get as much emotional value out of a 2000 year old resurrection story as they do from a good spiritual moment they have this week in church.

Fourth belief: our religion demands that we accept certain virtues as being 'good'. We work toward being virtuous our entire lives, without ever fully achieving 'goodness'. Still, we are obligated to keep trying. Our understanding of those virtues affects how we relate to other people. It also affects our political opinions. When you believe that God is compassionate and loves justice, you have to support policies that promote justice. When you believe you are supposed to be non-judgmental, you have to support policies that don't tell people how to live their lives. On the other hand, when you believe in virtues like temperance, humility and charity, you have to support policies that will promote these virtues without requiring all people to be virtuous.

You might be wondering what this discourse on personal belief, virtue, politics and public policy has to do with airplane hijackings, undercover investigations and an impending murder. The answer is simple: everything. Because religion determined how I responded to the mess I found myself in before this case was over. And, of course, my religious opinions caused me to do something that made the whole mess get much, much worse before it finally was resolved. That is what happens when you start letting your religion influence your behavior: you get into trouble.

CHAPTER 4. ED STAYS UNDERCOVER

The next morning I went out onto the deck to take a deep breath of fresh morning air. Betty was worried about the cats.

"Don't let the cats out on the deck. Bucky will jump off."

"Okay," I replied. The fool cat might jump off, but he was more likely to get on the roof since the stepladder was still on the porch from when I had changed the light bulb. I should have brought it in, but the weather had been nice and it seemed like a lot of trouble.

That day I was resolved to do a better job running my little lift truck. Those rough necks had razzed me enough; I would show them even a silver-haired geek could play a useful role on a construction site if he tried hard enough.

The first load was delivered to the floor tillers in a business-like way. The second load was delivered to them almost before they were done laying the tile from the first load. Still, they called me a few impolite names.

The third time I was faster yet, and I managed to deliver the load before the fourth man got to his feet. I dumped it, whirled around, and goosed the little motor. The tires spun for a second then we shot over toward the stack at twice the rate of the speed with which I had begun the morning.

I scooped up the load then raced back toward the floor tile crew. As I approached them, I slammed on the brakes, slid onto the newly laid tile, and spilled the load. Then some serious cursing ensued with you-know-who as the unhappy center of attention.

The foreman came over to calm the situation down. After sorting out the facts, he told everybody to take a break then glumly took me aside.

"Look, Shoemaker," he said. "You've created a problem for me. I know why you're here. But those guys know you're no good at driving the lift. If I don't take you off of it, they are going to wonder about it. Heck, they expect me to fire you right now, which is exactly what I would do to one of them if he screwed up like this."

"I see your point," I said. "Why don't you have me drive the lift over on the warehouse side of the building? If I can take loads to people who aren't in such a hurry, I'm sure I won't cause an accident. That will give me a chance to look over the situation back there."

The foreman considered the idea for a moment. "That's not my crew, but I think I can fix it with the warehouse foreman. Why don't you drive away like you've been fired, then come back in half an hour. You should park on the other side of the building. That way my team won't be able to see your car."

"No problem." It was a simple plan and it was bound to work like a charm.

Intending to implement it immediately I walked toward my car. The flooring crew was taking its break by their trucks, leaning against the beds and munching on snacks. They stared at me silently as I walked toward them. Bud couldn't help razzing me.

"Did old Buster give you the boot?"

"Yep. Guess I got off to a bad start."

"No kidding. You ain't had much practice driving a lift, have ya?

"Not a lot. Some."

"What's an old guy like you driving a lift for anyway? You sound like a college man."

"Laid off. Still have to pay the bills."

"Yeah, I can understand that. But maybe you better stay away from construction. Go work the counter at McDonald's or something."

"Maybe I'll do that."

Fatso turned away, stuffing the last of his snack into his mouth then guzzling from a large bottle of soda. He threw his empty wrapper through the open window of the truck, where it joined a large file of similar items. No wonder he was so hefty; his snack probably contained about a thousand calories and it appeared that he was eating several snacks a day.

When I returned thirty minutes later, the crew was out of sight, no doubt hard at work on the floor. Circling the building, I parked at the end of another line of pickup trucks. The warehouse foreman saw me arrive, and came over to join me. He made no comments about the circumstances, just told me to start unloading a semi. "Bring down a load and I will tell you where to take it. Then go get another load and we'll do it again," he directed.

"No problem," I replied.

Driving the lift was fun, though I almost tipped it over going into and out of the semi trailer. The warehouse foreman just shook his head in disgust, probably wondering about whether the company would get sued if I broke my neck. The truth was, though I enjoyed driving the lift, I wasn't really very good at it.

As the day wore on, I learned where the different products were being stored in the warehouse. The warehouse had been constructed first, with the builders moving toward the front of the retail part of the store. At that point in time, one crew was laying floor tile, while another followed along arranging the shelving. Out in the front of the floor tile crew, another team was putting down plywood to serve as a base for the tile.

In the warehouse, the arrangement of products was logical. Kids toys were grouped together, home appliances together, clothing in the same area, and food items that were packaged but still perishable went in the back of the warehouse, as far from the loading dock as possible. I supposed it made sense to keep them away from the open door, because that kept them out of the sun. However, it also located them near to where the construction teams were working. Maybe I was being a bit over-hasty but I already had some suspects in mind for being the likely snack food thieves. The warehouse foreman told me the tiling crew was a bunch of roughnecks who had bad reputations, especially Bud Miller. Good old Bud was my number one suspect for this investigation. If anybody was stealing junk food, it had to be Bud.

CHAPTER 5. THAR SHE BLOWS!

That evening the weather remained near-perfect. My deck practically begged me to park myself on it, light up my pipe, put my feet up, and start studying the documents that had appeared from nowhere. Pushing the stepladder to one side, I got comfortable and started reading. When my wife, Betty, got home, I took a break to share a salad with her (Betty could make salad taste good, which to my way of thinking is a rare talent). After the meal, I planned to go back onto the deck for my snooping exercise. Of course, I intended to return the briefcase to its rightful owner, but until I read further I would not know who the rightful owner was (or so my excuse was framed). Even so, my time with the documents would have to be brief or their owner might feel I had crossed the line between procrastination and theft.

The salad was excellent, as expected. Even Bucky, the fat cat, liked to stick his head into one of Betty's salads. As I was engrossed in my salad bowl, Betty had a question for me.

"What are you getting me for our anniversary," she asked innocently.

Alarm bells went off in my head. "Umm, I haven't decided."

"Did you remember that our anniversary was this weekend?"

"I knew it was coming up soon."

'You forgot our anniversary!"

"No, I knew it was around this time of year. You know, spring."

"Well, what are you going to get me?"

"I haven't decided. What would you like me to get you?" Later, I realized this was the question she was maneuvering me into asking. Of course, that did not mean she intended to answer it.

"Well, I don't know. You could get me perfume."

"Okay, I'll get you perfume."

"You never got me an expensive ring, you know."

"Eh?"

"Why didn't you ever get me an expensive ring?"

"You would just throw it in a drawer. What good is that?"

"Other wives have expensive rings. Don't you love me?

"Of course I love you!"

"You're a cheapskate. You would rather keep your money than spend it on me."

"If I spent a lot of money on a ring, it would just postpone the day when we can pay off our mortgage." This was a logical statement. It was also the wrong thing to say.

A few minutes later I escaped back out onto the deck to read those documents. Smoke may have been rising from my scorched feet, since Betty certainly had been holding them to the fire for the last few minutes. I collapsed into my wicker chair with a sigh.

Unfortunately, the post-prandial perusal proved to be brief. My cell phone rang with bad news: a major fire had occurred at a friend's home. Betty and I jumped into the car and ran over there.

At this point, a little background is in order. The previous year I had been involved in a little investigation of a research project involving psychiatric patients. Unfortunately, one of the patients had been found dead under suspicious circumstances. Specifically, he was found in a freezer that I had been sitting on. Trust me when I say we don't have to time to review that entire story right here.

Suffice it to say that when the investigation was over I found myself the director of a private foundation devoted to providing assistance to people afflicted with serious and persistent mental illness. One of my first acts was to provide funds for the purchase of mobile homes for a few people. One person received as a home a metal storage container that had been fit with a bathroom and other improvements. The owner of the storage container can be called Sherlock Holmes, since I should not use his actual name.

The phone call was from Doc Watson, a member of our board of directors who also had spent more than his share of time as a psychiatric inpatient. Doc had reported that Sherlock's place had become a raging inferno. While this concerned us a great deal, since Betty and I liked Sherlock, it did not surprise us greatly. The reason Sherlock was living in a storage canister instead of a mobile home was because we started him with a mobile home but he accidentally burned it down; Sherlock had a problem with accidental fires. We had hoped the storage canister was relatively inflammable. Apparently, we were overly optimistic.

When we arrived at Sherlock's place, or what was left of it, we were surprised to see that the fire was already out. We got out of the car and walked around the emergency vehicles to arrive at the site of the fire, with our mouths hanging open in shock; Sherlock's home was completely gone. Doc Watson was there, so I asked how the canister could have burned so completely,

"It didn't just burn, man, it was a fireball."

"A fireball?"

"Yeah. There was a *whump* and a giant fireball just went up into the sky."

Doc could see that I was inclined to doubt the accuracy of his report, so he gestured toward a nearby tree. Suspended by its branches was a sheet of corrugated metal, scorched black and buckled. A few small branches around it were burned off.

"Geeze," I said with awe. Then I wondered if there would be anything left of Sherlock to bury.

While we stood there bemused, watching the fireman hose off the black spot on the ground, a couple of police detectives we knew well came up to us.

The first to speak was Sergeant Broder. He nodded at us. "Professor Shumacher. Dr. Schumacher. How are you folks this evening?" Broder's partner, Sergeant Schmidt, stood by silently.

"We would be better if this hadn't happened," was my reply.

"Did you know the person who lived here?"

"Yes. Sherlock Holmes. The foundation I direct purchased this place for him."

Broder blinked, but did not ask me why a foundation would make a disabled person live in a storage container. "We are still gathering information, but as you know when someone dies, we have to interview anyone who has background on the case."

"I understand."

"Then, we will be in touch soon. Possibly tomorrow." Broder nodded to Doc Watson, whom he seemed to know, then he and Schmidt moved on to talk with the firemen.

"Well, Doc," I said, "this is a bummer. You doin' okay?"

"Yeah, I'm okay. But you know, me and Sherlock went way back. Things won't be the same without him."

'I know you did."

"It's hard to believe he's gone. You know, that guy could run like a rabbit. I didn't think anything would ever catch up to him."

"You want to come over to our place and have a drink?"

"Nah. Thanks anyway. I think I'll just go home and have a smoke." Doc was not talking about tobacco, I was pretty sure. He knew Betty and I would not be comfortable with illegal activities in our home. He was a sensitive and polite fellow on matters such as that. "I need to call some people and tell 'em what's happened," he said. "I'll let you know about the funeral and so on when I have more information." Doc wandered away, looking lost. His tall skinny frame was bent, as he walked with his head down.

"Poor Doc," Betty said sympathetically.

"Yep. This is rough on him."

We went back home at that point. There was no point in hanging around what had once been a man's home, but now was nothing more than a vacant lot with a black spot on the ground marking where good-natured Sherlock had once   entertained   his   friends.

CHAPTER 6. "THIS WAS NO ACCIDENT. IT WAS MURDER!"

The next day, I strolled down to the convenience store for the morning papers, as I did every morning. The coffee was brewing while I took that little walk, and it was ready to pour when I came back up the stairs. Betty liked me to bring her the coffee and a paper in the mornings before she got ready for her job in the clinic. She was a physician, and needed to relax when at home because she never had a chance after she got to work. She got the Milwaukee paper and I took the local paper, sitting down with it in my Morris chair. My cat, Fritter, sat down to watch me read while Betty's cat, Bucky, sprawled on the bed with her.

The front page story was about a plane that was hijacked between Madison and Milwaukee. The hijacker had held up the passengers with, of all things, a water pistol filled with indelible ink, then leaped out of the plane carrying a bunch of ladies' purses. What made this story even more interesting was the location; the thief bailed out somewhere in the sky over Fort Atkinson. I wondered if the leather satchel that I found on my deck had started out on that plane. That theory of its origins fit as well as any.

Since I was eager to finish the undercover job so that I could study the contents of the satchel, I decided driving a fork lift was no longer necessary. Instead, I resolved to "shake the tree," as we investigators like to say. The best method of tree-shaking is to act like you know more than you know, hoping that the perpetrator will be goaded into action.

My method for doing that was to drive over to the construction site, pull up next to the pickup trucks, then start peering into their windows. Within a few minutes a small group of tile-experts were standing around me in a semi-circle. Their craggy heads sat atop broad shoulders. Their bulging forearms were connected to big hard looking fists, each of which was carrying a good-sized hammer. Yes, there was no doubt; tree-shaking could be amazingly effective.

"Watch doin' there, grampa?" asked their ringleader and my number one suspect, Bud Miller.

"Just looking around a little."

"And why would you be looking around our trucks? Answer me that, why doncha?" Miller pulled a tart out of his pocket, ripped it open, and took a large bite.

"Well, it's like this. I heard some stuff was disappearing from the warehouse I wondered if maybe you guys knew something about it."

Miller's face grew red as he munched the tart. He was beginning to get angry. "We don't know crap about it and we don't appreciate you nosing around our trucks. Maybe you need some kinda lesson about minding your own business." He whirled and swung the hammer at my car, breaking out a parking light. "Darn!" he said. "My hand musta slipped. Sorry about that, gramps." Bud laughed, then frowned at me. "It's a good thing for you it didn't slip in the direction of your head," he hissed. He stuffed his gooey tart wrapper into my shirt pocket. "Here, have a little going away present. Now, go away and don't come back."

He had made his point, so he let me go past him and get into my car. As I drove away, I could not help smiling. Yes, he had made his point. He also had promoted himself from number one suspect to guilty-as-hell.

From that point on, I was sure of the case. What I was not sure about was how I was going to prove it. A truck cab full of junk food wrappers would not prove a thing. He could have gotten them anywhere.

Wait, I thought. That's old-fashioned thinking. These big box retail stores have great inventory systems. What if the wrapper Miller stuffed into my pocket was marked with a number? What if that particular tart had come from the warehouse instead of some convenience store down the road? Miller's fingerprints were on the wrapper. Maybe I had all the evidence I was going to need.

Naturally, I was feeling pretty pleased with myself. The case was solved already. That should be worth a bonus. As I nosed the car into my driveway I noticed Broder and Schmidt leaning against their blue sedan, parked out by the street. When they saw me, they began walking toward the condo. That brought me down to earth; they were here, as promised, to talk about Sherlock's untimely death.

"Come on in, you guys," I offered, leading the way up the stairs.

They seated themselves on the couch while I parked in the usual spot: my Morris chair. With my feet on the ottoman, I was ready to answer their questions, I thought.

Schmidt started first. "Who do you know that can get high-explosives, Schumacher?" she demanded.

"Eh?"

"I know you can't, but a crackpot like you has crackpot friends. So which of them got the explosives?"

"What are you talking about?"

Broder broke in at this point. "Professor, the fire we looked at last night was not an accident. Residue was found from a very powerful explosive not available to the general public."

"Somebody murdered Sherlock?" This made no sense. Sherlock was more than a bit odd, but he never threatened anyone. I told Broder and Schmidt that and they seemed to believe I was sincere.

"Professor, be that as it may. Someone did it. They must have had a reason." Broder stood up on that note. "If you think of anything that might be relevant, please call us right away." The two of them left me sitting stunned in my chair. Nobody would want to kill Sherlock. But someone did. It made no sense at all.

In situations like this one, I had always found it to be helpful to make a list of what I knew and what I didn't. The list looked like this.

1. Somebody killed Sherlock by blowing up his trailer.
2. Sherlock was harmless, but
3. Sherlock must have made some nasty enemies.

Wait a minute, I thought. Maybe it was a case of mistaken identity. Sherlock was not the kind of guy to make nasty enemies. It had to be some kind of giant mistake.

After reaching this conclusion, I felt much better.

CHAPTER 7. THE DEAD MAN ALOFT

When you need to clear your mind, and the weather is nice, take a walk. That was the motto that had served me well for years, so off I went, down the stairs, out the door, and down the street. Thirty minutes later I was sitting in a booth in my favorite coffee shop, the McDonalds on Main Street.

The leather satchel had been clutched in my hand all the way over to McDonalds, since my intention was to spend an hour studying its contents. As it turned out, the information on those documents was worth the trouble of carrying the satchel on my walk.

The documents, when arranged chronologically, detailed the gradual development of an agreement involving several major food producers and the federal government. The agreement benefited the food industry in amounts even those guys could not estimate, because too many zeros were involved. The agreement also was rotten. Here are the essential points of the agreement.

First point: since the food industry was feeling a little exposed on the issue of the worldwide obesity epidemic, its leaders felt it was time to go on the offensive with a misinformation campaign, the major elements of which involved telling Americans in particular and the world in general that people did not consume too many calories, they just exercised too little. The large agricultural companies, the distributors, and the restaurants had too much at stake to allow consumers to get the idea that they should cut back on calories. Calories were profits.

Second point: the federal government agreed to support this position in every way, including modification of the health advice provided to the public and applying pressure to the World Health Organization to do the same. Unstinting support for candidates backed by the administration would be its reward.

Third point: the federal government would assist the food industry in suppressing research evidence about food addiction. The evidence was shocking. High calories foods were as habit forming as cigarettes. People who became addicted to sugar highs could be counted on to continue over-consuming calories to an extent that was almost unbelievable. Hiding this fact was essential to the food industry, because it wanted to insure that children were addicted to high-calorie foods at an early age, thus ensuring their value as customers for the entire lives, lives that would be much shorter than they otherwise would have been because they were going to die early of obesity-related diseases.

This plot was dazzling in its iniquity and also its boldness. On the other hand, I thought, was it any different from what the tobacco industry had done?

Of more immediate concern was finding an answer to this question: what was I going to do with these documents? Giving them back to the food industry executive who lost them was not an option. My hands shook as I stacked up the papers, put them back in the satchel then slid the satchel down snugly between my leg and the wall. My brain was frozen by the enormity of what I had found and the responsibility that had literally fallen into my life.

As I sipped the fine brew and contemplated nothing much at all, an old acquaintance slipped into the seat across from me.

"Skip Cavanaugh! You old son of a gun!" We shook hands heartily and exchanged grins. Skip was with the Department of Homeland Security, a fact he would firmly deny. In fact, Skip was so expert at being a spook that after the last time he was in town I was the only one who remembered he had ever been around. In fact, I was the only one who even believed that he existed at all. Even Betty claimed I had dreamed up the man's existence, and she should have known better than to question the accuracy of my perceptions and instincts on matters relating to murder and spies.

This little trip down memory lane caused me to realize something: Skip was here for a reason, no doubt one that the ACLU would not find acceptable.

"So, Skip, what brings you back to Fort? Are you causing trouble again?"

Skip's face turned serious. "This time I'm here on an assignment that is quite a bit trickier than the last one. And I'm sure I don't have to tell you that we never had this conversation."

"Same old Skip."

"Are you carrying around any hard feelings about the last time I was here?"

"Nah, Skip. I know you saved my bacon. But everybody thought I was a nut after that. You can't blame me for being a little unhappy."

Skip smiled at me with a twinkle in his eye. "People would not have believed you were a nut unless maybe they had reason to," he said gently.

I had to laugh. "Okay, it's not all your fault that people think I'm a nut. Well, since that's out of the way, what kind of trouble are you going to get me into this time?"

"This is not about you, Ed." Skip was not smiling. "This is about the explosion that happened last night. I understand your friend's place was destroyed."

"Yes, that's right. He was a harmless guy, but the cops tell me that it was murder. I just can't believe it."

"I know what information the police have, and it's accurate as far as it goes. Somebody with unusual access to explosives used them to commit murder. We think we know who did it, and we think we know why."

"Great! That means you're going to nail the bastards."

Skip averted his eyes for moment, clearly thrown off by my outburst.

"Well, the least you can do is tell me why they killed poor Sherlock."

Skip hesitated then asked, "Did you read about the plane that was hijacked?"

"Sure, what about it?"

"Don't ask for too many details, but the hijacker made off with something more valuable than a few purses."

My heart stopped. Was somebody important looking for the documents that at that moment was resting between my leg and the wall?

"Like what?" I asked innocently.

"I can't tell you that. Let's just say the hijacker was a member of a terrorist group and leave it go at that."

"Next you'll try to sell me the Brooklyn Bridge. I don't believe this for a second. But put that aside."

"It's true. The terrorist organization calls itself CRAPO."

"No shit? But what does it have to do with Sherlock?"

"The person who hijacked that plane was traced by agents to Fort. Those agents connected your friend Sherlock to the terrorist group. He also fit the physical description of the hijacker.

Now I was angry. "Wait a minute! For one thing, Sherlock was a complete coward as well as being nonviolent. He ran like a rabbit at the first hint of possible trouble. He would never have hijacked an airplane. Second, it sounds like you are telling me agents of our own government are blowing up citizens who are suspected of having committed crimes. Please don't tell me we've come to that!"

Skip held his hand up to stop my tirade. "Hold on, Ed. I called these people agents. I did not say they were government agents. They were private security agents and they greatly exceeded their authority. We are not going to allow guys like this to get away with murder, at least not without the proper authorizations. I'm here to catch them and to take them away to some place quiet for questioning. Then we will decide what to do with them."

Then Skip really surprised me. "Look, Ed," he said. "I know you don't think Holmes had anything to do with the hijacking. But we looked into his background, and it turns out he was a ranger before he had his psychotic break. He parachuted out of planes hundreds of times. And he saw some serious action. He was decorated for bravery under fire."

My jaw dropped open. Sherlock had been a war hero?

Skip shook his head to clear it. "We've gotten off track. This is not what I sat down to talk about with you."

Skip took a deep breath then continued with what he had to say. "Look, Ed. There is every reason to believe Holmes had the … item … that was taken from the plane. I need you to tell me where he might have hidden it. Because you can be sure that nobody would have blown up his home if there was any chance that the, hmm, item… was still inside."

I stared into the bottom of my coffee cup for a moment then looked him in the eye. "Skip, Sherlock did not do this. That means he did not hide whatever it is anywhere. Somebody killed the wrong guy." Then I

110

grabbed the satchel, got up and left. As I walked home, I completed the statement in my mind: "They should have killed me instead." After all, I was the one who had the, hmm, item.

So, the man who fell to earth after the hijacking was also my friend who was killed when his home exploded. My dead friend had fallen out of the sky. None of this made any sense at all.

CHAPTER 8. SHERLOCK WAS ROBIN HOOD?

When I got back to the condo, I called Betty's cousin Andrew and suggested we go out for a beer that evening. He could tell from the sound of my voice that it was important. We set it up for Bienfang's place, where the beer was affordable. I had a feeling I would need a lot of it.

The rest of the day I sat on the deck smoking my pipe and moping. I could not get over the terrible feeling that I was somehow responsible for Sherlock's death. If not responsible, then somehow he had died in my place. I owed him...something. But I was not sure what I had to do to settle the debt.

When Betty got home I told her I was meeting Andrew for a beer later. We ate our dinner in silence.

Then she asked me what was bothering me.

"Nothing."

"Something is bothering you. Either that or you're depressed. Are you depressed?

"No, I'm not depressed."

"Yes, you are. I can tell."

"Well, I'm not."

She decided to change tactics. "How is your new job going?" Betty knew I had gone undercover at the construction site.

"Oh, it's pretty much finished."

"Finished! Already? How did it turn out?"

"Oh, some of the guys were stealing junk food. I figured out who it was. I even got some evidence."

"Evidence, just like a real detective?" Betty knew that, even in my most grandiose delusions, I did regard myself as a real detective.

"Yup, real evidence."

"That's wonderful dear. I'm so proud of you."

Her praise cheered me up, as it always did. Shortly after that it was time to meet Andrew.

We sat in the back room at Bienfang's place. Andrew bought the first round, then asked me about my undercover investigation. I gave him a full account.

"Which reminds me," I said. "What should I do with this wrapper?" Andrew was a state investigator. He would know what to do next.

He sighed, staring morosely at the wadded up wrapper. "Have you been handling that a lot?" he asked.

"Nope. It's been in my pocket all day."

"Well, I suggest you put it into a baggie then Fedex it to your contracting officer at the insurance company. Let them get the forensics done."

"Good idea." I stuffed the wrapper back in my pocket.

'You're lucky those guys didn't beat the crap out of you."

"Yeah, it was kind of a close call there for a minute. But it worked out okay."

"Isn't that why you called me? I thought you must be in hot water over the investigation."

"No. I called you about something a lot more serious than that."

Andrew put his beer down and stared at me while I told the story. Then he got up and bought us two more. They serve tiny little beers in that place.

"Let me see if I have this straight," he said after taking a gulp. "A bunch of incriminating documents just happens to fall on your porch, after a plane is hijacked. Various shadowy secret agents think your friend Sherlock Holmes was the hijacker so they blow up his house, I guess to cover up their tracks. But what they really want is the briefcase that fell on your deck. Then a guy who doesn't exist who you thought you saw back before your breakdown comes to see you and explains all this to you. Have I got it right?"

"Somehow I don't think you believe me."

"If I believed you, both of us would be crazy."

"Instead of just me, you mean."

"I don't want to hurt your feelings, Ed, but this is too much."

I didn't answer him, being engrossed in my beer.

"I was sorry to hear about Sherlock," Andrew offered. "That must have upset you."

"You really think I've lost it."

"You have to admit it sounds crazy, even for you."

"Okay, do this much for me. Put out a few feelers and see if you hear that something about the hijacking is being kept from the press. See if the police haven't been told to be on the lookout for something other than an airborne purse-snatcher."

Andrew just shook his head. "Take my advice and go to bed. You need to rest up. A lot."

We ended the evening on that unhappy note. Back at the condo, I went back out on the deck and smoked my pipe in the dark. Betty came out and tried to talk to me, but finally gave up and went to bed.

I forced myself to reconsider my belief that Sherlock was not the hijacker. If shadowy agents inside and out of government believed he did it, maybe he did. My knowledge of the guy told me he was incapable of making the detailed plans that would have been required, even he wasn't afraid of his own shadow. The only way he could have done something that frightened him was if he thought it would be very important in helping someone else.

Maybe that was it. Maybe the so-called terrorist group was actually engaged in a good cause, and they recruited

Sherlock. Would that make Sherlock sort of a Robin Hood of the skies?

That thought made me feel a little better. I rushed off to bed before the idea faded away completely.

CHAPTER 9. ANDREW EATS CROW

The next evening, Andrew and I met at Sal's. He had called me, said he had some information for me, and suggested we get together. He sounded very serious, which I took as a good sign. At least he wasn't laughing at me.

This time I bought the first round. Andrew asked for one of the goofy cow beers from New Glarus while I had a Bud. Miller High Life was good too, but since the South Africans bought the brewery, my enthusiasm for the brew had waned a bit.

Andrew had to eat some crow. He came right out with it.

"Ed, I did a little checking and it turns out some of what you were saying actually was true."

"Really? Pardon me if I don't act surprised."

"Okay, I guess I owe you an apology. You are not completely crazy. Until we know more I won't back down any more than that."

"Good enough. I can wait."

"Here are the facts. An all-points went out on the hijacker right after he left the airplane. He was described as armed and dangerous, which is a little odd, because nobody saw any weapons other than the water pistol."

"That sounds suspicious right there. What else?"

"Traffic on other channels suggested that some of the spookier agencies were looking into the case, even though the national security implications of a water pistol don't seem very obvious to me, or anybody else I spoke to."

"Ah ha!"

"Finally, I was able to find out something about that terrorist organization you said was called CRAPO."

Andrew hesitated, taking a swig from his cow beer.

"Don't stop now."

"Okay," he continued. "CRAPO stands for Citizens Resistance Against Promotion of Obesity. They claim that big corporations are deliberately promoting addiction to high-calorie foods, thus causing the worldwide obesity epidemic. CRAPO is a relatively unknown group, but so was PITA before animal rights became a highly publicized issue."

"Let me see if I have this right. The behavior of the spook agencies suggests that something more important than ladies' purses disappeared off that plane. Furthermore, the spooks seem to think that CRAPO might have been behind the hijacking. Putting two and two together, whatever was lost that had national security implications was something that CRAPO would think was important. For example, it might be documents proving that CRAPO is right in its claims about a corporate conspiracy to promote addictive foods. Which is just exactly what I told you was in those documents. So, do you believe me now?"

"Calm down, Ed. I'm sorry I didn't believe in those documents. You have to admit that what you were saying was pretty far-fetched."

"The big question in my mind is this: what do I do with the darn things?"

"Well, don't look at me. I can't think of any place I could pass them where they wouldn't end up being passed to a spook agency, which then would bury them forever."

"That is not acceptable. What the corporations are doing is criminal, almost on the level of mass murder."

"Now wait a minute, Ed. No matter how habit forming high-calorie food is, people could break the habit if they wanted to. We all have choices. We don't have to eat everything in sight."

"You can't be telling me I should look the other way on this!"

"I'm telling you that some powerful groups have shown how far they are willing to go to bury this. If they find out you have those documents, you are the one who is going to get buried."

"I have a responsibility here, Andrew. It was my bad luck that put those documents on my deck. But now I have to do the right thing. The fact is, governments exist to protect people, not to help corporations maximize profits at the expense of the citizens."

"Are you sure the government is supposed to protect the public from every unhealthy product people want to buy? That sounds like Big Brother to me."

"The government shouldn't interfere in the market unless the companies go too far in pursuit of profit. In this case, they have crossed the line. The companies crossed the line so far they can't even see it anymore."

Andrew nodded his head. "You're right. I know you're right. But I'm having trouble understanding why smart people at the top of the government and big companies would do something this outrageous. What's wrong with them?"

"You know what's wrong with them. Power and money are corrupting influences and they deal with both in gigantic quantities every day. That would be like Superman handling kryptonite. Power and money have poisoned them."

"If what you say is right, then governments and corporations will always get out of hand sooner or later."

"And they always do. It's inevitable. That's why we have to keep both government and corporations as small as possible: so they can do some good without become so corrupt and dangerous."

"How can the government do its job if it's small?"

"Assuring a decent minimum quality of life doesn't require big government. We don't have to have expensive welfare programs if we keep the cost of living low. We just have to set some limits with our planning and zoning policies and our local ordinances."

Andrew wasn't buying my argument. "The corporations will always be big," he said. "Mass production is more efficient, and that means bigger companies will have an edge."

"They have an edge because the government gives them a lot of breaks. Efficiency in production can be reached in smaller factories than most people realize. The factories get bigger because executives like big budgets and because the government gives them bigger tax breaks if they claim they are bringing in more jobs."

"Even if all that is true, what makes you think the voters will want to keep the cost of living low? Most people want bigger incomes so that they can buy bigger houses and bigger cars."

"You're right, Andrew. Most people don't really value humility and frugality. Most are materialistic and short sighted. But even the dumbest would like to see his taxes cut. And most people get tired of working all the time. If some local official points out that we could all work less if the cost of living was lower, then, sooner or later, some people are going to think that sounds good. The truth is, economic growth has mixed benefits. In some ways, it hurts us more than it helps us."

"You can't force people to believe what you believe."

"No, but it should be possible to give people a choice. If you want to be a materialist and try to get rich, go for it. But the other choice should be possible too: working less hard and still having a decent life. By letting the capitalists call all the shots, we seem to have lost our ability to make the second choice. Everybody has to work like crazy just to pay their taxes."

"So you think this business with the corporate obesity cover up is just a predictable case of capitalism gone out of control."

"Damn right. And the cure is not socialism, either. We have to shrink both the government and the corporations.'

"And what if there is no way to do that?"

"Then a few of us will have to make little islands of sanity in a vast sea of worldly evil, that's what. It won't be the first time in history that has been necessary. Fact is, the world is just naturally corrupt."

Andrew did not want to believe the world was all that bad, because he was a naturally optimistic guy. Even so, he raised his glass in a toast. "Down with corruption," he said.

"Down with corruption," I responded. We clinked our glasses together and drank them down. Then it was time to go home.

Without realizing it, I had resolved not to let those documents get in the hands of their original owners. Now that I had voiced my political opinions, I was committed to fighting the conspiracy that had accidentally been unmasked. Andrew had figured that out, and he was worried about how it would turn out. What he did not realize, because I had not told him, was that the political arguments I had given him were all based on the religious convictions I had worked out for myself a few days before. See what I mean? Once you start letting your religion influence your behavior, you are bound to get into trouble.

CHAPTER 10. THE TEMPTATION

The next day, after Betty went to work, my contracting officer at the insurance office called to ask if I was making progress. The cats and I were playing with an artificial mouse when he called. I promised him that I was hoping for a break in the case soon, but could not provide details as yet. Leaving the impression that I was hard at work, I managed to get a couple more days of pay out of the job.

Later, when I was out on the deck sipping the coffee and watching the world go by, our downstairs neighbor, Emily Eberhardt, came back from walking her dog Spot.

"Emily!" I yelled. "Come on up for some fresh coffee, if you want."

She came up and sat with me for awhile, so I told her a bit about the food industry conspiracy. She was outraged.

"But you be careful," she warned. "These big companies will stop at nothing. They have a lot at stake and if they realize you are an obstacle, they will come after you."

"Aw, Emily," I groaned. "Don't start. Sure, they'll be upset if they get caught. But once everything goes public, there's nothing they can do."

"You mark my words," she responded with a stern look. "Nothing has been made public yet. Until then, they can do whatever they want and probably get away with it."

"Okay, you have a point. I will get rid of those documents as quickly as I can."

Emily went back downstairs and I started thinking hard about who should get the documents. Should I mail them to the New York Times? Or maybe I should try to find those CRAPO guys.

At that moment the door bell rang. It was my favorite spook Skip.

Without preamble, he said, "Ed, we need to take a ride."

"Yeah? Where?"

"Don't worry, we're just going up the street to the Holiday Inn Express."

We drove over to the Inn and walked up the stairs to a second floor room. A young man opened the door and waved us inside. A distinguished woman in a business suit sat in an upholstered chair.

The young man extended his hand for a shake, saying his name was Arnie. He did not mention the woman. Apparently, she was there to observe and intercede only if necessary.

Arnie led me over to the small table in the room, where he seated me. Skip stood in front of the door, arms folded in front of him in what the Army taught me was the 'parade rest' position.

Arnie offered me a drink, which I declined, then seated himself in the other table chair and crossed his legs, leaning back in a relaxed posture that no doubt was intended to indicate self-assurance.

"It's so nice to meet you, Professor Schumacher. We've heard a lot about you."

"I deny everything."

Arnie chuckled. "No, no, you are an accomplished man. A doctorate from a major university, a career in research, many publications. Anyone would be proud." He beamed at me. 'Of course, things have not gone so well recently. You have been in trouble with the police on numerous occasions. Your business ventures have not exactly been big winners for you. And now you seem to be entangled in something that is way over your head."

"And what would that be?" I asked innocently.

Arnie laughed. "I didn't expect to find that you had such a fine sense of humor, Professor. Or may I call you Ed?"

"Ed is fine."

"Well, Ed, all humor aside, this is not the time to be coy. You probably can tell us where to look for something that Mr. Holmes hid away before his unfortunate accident. We want you to tell us where it might be. Retrieving it is of the utmost importance."

"I have no idea what you're talking about," was my reply. "Well, it's been nice meeting you," I gestured toward the silent woman, "and not meeting your boss, but I have things to do, places to go. You know how it is: busy, busy, busy," I stood up and headed for the door.

"Wait," the woman said, though she didn't need to, since Skip had not moved a hair and he was blocking the door.

"Professor, speak with me for a moment." She had a quiet commanding presence that Arnie no doubt yearned to acquire. I turned toward her before realizing that I was already following her orders.

"We represent powerful interests. These interests have resources that can do a great deal of good in the world. With the backing of those interests, you could do a great deal of good in the world."

"What are you proposing?"

"What do you want? Have you ever thought about owning a newspaper?"

"Management gets to be boring after about two days."

"But you would enjoy writing those editorials every day. You could delegate the management part." When I did not respond she turned toward the window, drawing the curtain open.

"You can see a long distance from here," she observed. "This is one of the taller buildings in town and we are at a higher elevation than most of the city."

"Yes, we are in one of the highest places in Fort Atkinson. But it's only the second floor. What is your point?"

"You like small towns, Professor Schumacher. You would really enjoy being an important person in this town. For example, with the right backing, you could become the mayor. Or you could start an investment company, making deals in real estate or any other sector in the local economy. This would make you even more powerful than if you went into politics, and much richer."

I looked out over the town, which really was very dear to my heart, and I thought about what she was offering. Then I shook my head.

"Nice try, but I prefer to go it alone. That way I have a better chance of staying honest." With that, I headed for the door. Skip blocked my way, looking for a sign from the woman. She must have given it, because he stepped aside and I left. Since it was only a short walk from home, I didn't hang around to wait for him to offer me a lift.

A few minutes after I got home, my cell phone rang. It was Skip.

"Get out of there," he said. "*Now.*"

"What are you talking about?"

"Ed, listen to me. I have this one chance to warn you. We're coming for you right away. You will be arrested on a national security charge, held in secret without trial until they learn what they want to know."

"They can't scare me!" I blustered.

"Ed, do you know what they do with a rubber hose?"

"Thanks for the call, Skip. I'm getting out of here. Fast."

CHAPTER 11. THE ESCAPE

Sirens wailed loudly, then tires screeched. Peeking through the glass door by the deck, I could see Broder and Schmidt standing by the door. The bell rang, but they did not wait long after that. Broder pulled out his gun to shoot the lock.

At that moment, Emily stepped from her condo, which was right below ours. "What are you people doing?" she demanded.

"Stay out of this ma'am," Broder said. "Police business."

Then shot my doorknob.

"Sic 'em, Spot!" Emily shouted. Barking proved Spot could follow instructions. During the distraction I stepped out onto my deck and climbed the ladder to the roof. As I scrambled over the shingles, I wondered how I was going to explain all this to Betty.

Crab-walking over the crest of the roof, I lost my footing and slid over the edge to land on the deck of a second-floor condo. As I lay there stunned but otherwise unhurt, the sliding glass door opened and a well-rounded buxom woman in a fluffy robe was revealed.

"Don't this just beat all," she said. "Here I was just thinking about men and one appears on my deck."

"Hide me, please," I pleaded. "I'm being chased."

"Who is chasing you?"

"There isn't time to explain now."

"You better try, Buster."

"I have documents proving the food industry is conspiring with the government to promote consumption of high-calorie foods, leading to the obesity epidemic and millions of deaths worldwide."

At that moment we heard voices on the roof above us.

"Quick," she said. "Come inside."

She led me into her bedroom where a bottle of wine sat next to a double bed covered with a large mound of pillows. A bag of chips was on the nightstand.

"Get into the middle of the bed and lie flat. I'll cover you up."

This will never work, I thought, but followed the instructions anyway. It's a good thing I did, because the bed was a waterbed and I quickly sank deeply into its embrace. She piled pillows over my head and everything went dark. I could feel her arranging herself on top of me and pulling the quilt up over us.

At that moment my pursuers burst into the room. The woman shrieked convincingly.

"What are you people doing in my bedroom?" she demanded angrily, outrage dripping from every word.

"We're following someone."

"Well, you can see he's not in here. Get out!"

They left, making profuse apologies.

"Stay still for awhile" she whispered to me. "We better wait until they leave the building."

She shifted her position, trying to get more comfortable, I guessed. We lay there quietly for awhile then she began to squirm a little. A few minutes later, she got off the bed and pulled off the pillows. I followed suit, heading for the front door, which was at the bottom of the stairs. I opened it carefully, listening first then peered out. Before I slipped out, I looked back at my benefactor.

"Thanks," I said with feeling. "You saved my bacon."

"No problem," she said, with a big smile. "It was a pleasure to be of assistance, sir." She was giggling as she closed the door behind me.

126

As I stepped out on the sidewalk, an older woman in the doorway of the downstairs unit beckoned to me excitedly.

"Over here! Quick!"

When I trotted over to her, she said, "The cops are still in your place. You better hide in here."

She ushered me, then sat in a wooden chair at the kitchen table. A rifle was leaning against the wall, which she picked up and aimed casually at the door. "If those rats try to take you, they will get a fight from us! Have a seat, Ed. Emily told us all about your situation. You can count on us."

At that moment a door opened in the back of the condo and we could hear water running. A chubby elderly man emerged holding another rifle.

He gave me a big grin, saying, "You must be Ed. Welcome to our little home. Don't worry; we won't last those bastards get you." He shook hands vigorously. "My name is Bob. This here is Lucy." He seated himself at the table and aimed his rifle at the door also.

"Um, Bob, are you sure you want to get involved in this?" I asked him. "You could get into big trouble."

"Hell, yes we want to get involved. It's our duty as God-fearing Americans. See this gut?" He patted himself on his enormous belly. "I need to lose it but I can't. Those bastards who're after you got me hooked. It's time somebody stood up to 'em."

Lucy started dialing her telephone. She called Emily and somebody called Hilda, telling them to bring elements of a disguise for me to wear while making good my escape.

Emily arrived almost immediately, bringing Spot with her. Little Spot started jumping on me excitedly while Emily tried to calm him down. This was awkward, she was holding a shotgun in one hand.

Next Hilda arrived. Hilda was wearing a pink floppy hat and a lavender raincoat. When she took them off I realized Hilda was the woman who had hidden me in her water bed.

They quickly explained their plan. I was to wear the raincoat and hat and take Spot with me. It would like I was Hilda out walking a dog. All of them agreed that it was a good disguise.

A few minutes later, Spot and I were a block away from the building. When I looked back, I could see Skip standing on my deck looking in my direction. He gave no indication that he recognized me. With Skip there was no way of telling whether he had or he hadn't. That Skip was hard   to   figure.

CHAPTER 12. BUD KICKS BUTT

About six blocks farther along, I removed the disguise. I sensed that perhaps wearing it made me more conspicuous than not wearing it. Bundling the raincoat and hat under my arm, Spot and I kept walking. My problem at that point was that I had no idea where I should go.

Fifteen minutes later we arrived at the parking lot of the Sentry grocery store. As Spot and I crossed the pavement, a large pickup truck skidded to a stop in front of me. Three others quickly blocked all the directions of possible escape. Bud Miller and his buddies had caught up with me.

Bud and his crew got out of their trucks and crowded around me, shoving me back and forth.

"You sneak," Bud said. "The word around the site is that you were spying on us. The foreman said if anything else disappears, some people are going to get fired." He shoved me again. "Rats like you should get lessons in how to keep their mouths shut." He drew back his fist, intending to let me have a good one right in the face.

"Bud! I have your prints!" I burst out.

He hesitated.

"I got your prints off that wrapper you stuck into my shirt. The bar code on the wrapper shows it was from the batch that was stolen."

His eyes acquired a distant look. He was trying to remember what wrapper I was talking about.

"You do anything to me and you won't just get fired. You'll go down for a violent crime."

Bud lowered his fist.

"Look, Bud. I know what's going on here. You wouldn't be stealing junk food unless you were hooked on the stuff.

Bud's eyes shifted. He looked distinctly embarrassed.

"If you were going in to the robbery business, a tough guy like you wouldn't mess around with stealing junk food unless you were hooked on it."

The hefty guys crowding around could not resist voicing mutters of agreement.

"How do you think you got hooked on that stuff? Hell, you wouldn't be in this mess if the food industry wasn't pushing it on you. Betcha didn't know it was habit forming. They knew it, and they pushed it on you guys anyway. It's as bad as cigarettes."

Bud looked like he was going to cry. "Those lousy bastards," he groaned. "They got me hooked and now look at me." He looked down at his big belly. When he did, his double chin became a triple chin. "If I could get my hands on them, I would give 'em hell!" he snarled.

"Bud," I said gently. "I know how you can get even with them. Let's go get a brew and talk about it.

An hour later, Betty picked me and Spot up at Bienfang's. I was okay, but Spot was a little tipsy. When Betty got me home and we returned Spot to Emily, she demanded a full explanation. Naturally, I told her almost everything.

The next day, Skip called to tell me the heat was off. When I asked why, he said, "Let's just say that the people who were after you have bigger problems right at the moment."

He was certainly right about that. Two weeks of relative quiet were broken when the biggest story ever to hit Fort Atkinson broke out. Somebody had left two naked people tied up in front of the newspaper office.

Both appeared to have been force-fed high calorie food for a couple of weeks. Flabby skin hung down all around them. A sign was hung around the woman's neck that read: "This is what the food industry wants to happen to you."

A sign hung around the man's neck said, "Join CRAPO!"

CHAPTER 13. WHAT ABOUT SHERLOCK?

As I was taking my walk, I must have been unusually pre-occupied. When my right foot was supposed to hit the ground, it somehow missed. Next thing I knew, I was flat on my back on the pavement. Getting up was not too difficult. Thankfully, nothing hurt too much. I checked my ankle, my knee, my back and my neck. When I told Betty about it later, she said I must have jarred something loose, because she didn't believe anything I said happened after the fall. She also said I was in too good a mood, which wasn't normal and indicating that I must have banged my head on the sidewalk.

As I was checking myself for broken bones or other injuries a long-haired fellow with a beard walked up to me. I didn't pay much attention to him.

"Hey, Professor. Ain't you gonna say 'hi'?"

"Sherlock! My God! Is it really you?"

"Yeah, it's me."

"We thought you were dead!"

"So did I. It was cool, man." The bright sun was lighting up his face. He had never looked as happy in all the time I had known him.

"Where have you been all this time? Does Doc know you are okay?"

"Oh, sure, Doc has seen me. So have a few of the other guys. I wasn't sure whether you would see me or not."

"Heck, Sherlock – I'm always glad to see you."

"That's nice. I wanted to see you one more time before I took off."

"Took off? Where are you going?"

"You know how it is: places to go, things to do. It's time to move on to bigger and better things."

"How long will you be gone?"

"Can't say. But I'll see you guys again some day, when it's time."

"You'll be missed."

"Thanks, Professor. Hey, there was one thing I wanted to mention to you before I go."

"What's that, Sherlock?"

"Those ideas you have about religion. They ain't half bad. A lot of people might join the church if they thought about it they way you do."

"You really think so?"

"Yeah, I'm sure of it. I ain't saying you got it all right, or even half right. But it's close enough. And your ideas are simple, so the average person can understand them, if they want to. Maybe you should be a preacher."

"Nah, I'm not cut out for that. Can't remember names."

"Well, there's lots of ways to preach. You could do it writing. You could tell a story. Sometimes there's more truth in fiction than there is in a book of sermons."

"You might be right. Maybe that is how I can do a little good in the world."

"I'm sure of it."

"I'll think about writing some fiction."

"You do that. Hey, time for me to go."

"Before you take off, tell me something: did you have anything to do with that business on the airplane? Are you involved in some group that calls itself CRAPO?"

"Does it really matter?" he asked, giving me a direct look along with a small smile.

"Some people might think so."

"Then they can decide for themselves. Whatever they want to think is okay with me."

He was gone in a flash. One thing about Sherlock, he could always run like a rabbit.

"So, long, Sherlock," I said to the empty space where he had stood a moment before.

As I plodded home, I wondered how he had known what I was thinking about religion. I didn't remember telling anyone. Well, I was always both mouthy and forgetful, so probably I had voiced my arguments somewhere.

When and where that might have been always remained a mystery for me. That was okay, I have always loved a mystery, as most people do.

CHAPTER 13. CONCLUSION

The next few days went by quickly. Our cats, Fritter and Bucky, seemed to be unusually entertaining. They probably were picking up on Betty's excitement.

Betty said it was the best anniversary ever. I had given her a nice diamond ring, which she said she would wear all the time because there was no point in just throwing it into a drawer. We went to a live broadcast of her favorite public radio show in St. Paul, an event that made her almost deliriously happy.

"Did you like any of it?" she asked me on the way home.

"Of course, I did," I replied. "It was very professional. The music was great and it was funny."

"Then why did you fall asleep?"

"They turned down the lights. What did they expect was going to happen?"

"You didn't fall asleep when we went to the live broadcast of that Wisconsin public radio show," she observed.

"Those guys knew better than to turn the lights down."

"You are just biased in favor of Wisconsin."

Betty may have been right about that. People in Minnesota liked to think they were more sophisticated than their cousins in our state. I won't go so far as to say people who lived in the Twin Cities were stuck up. On the other hand, it had not escaped my attention that the boss at Minnesota Public Radio was paid double what the chancellor of University of Wisconsin was paid. People in the Cities might not be stuck up, but they did seem to think a lot of themselves.

When we got back from the Cities, several of us agreed to meet at Sal's to review the case. Emily Eberdardt was there, along with Andrew, Betty and I. I tried to reach Skip to invite him along, but was unable to reach him. I was pretty sure he would not have attended anyway, since keeping a low profile was his standard operating procedure.

We started out talking about what had been in the papers, all of which had been having a great time with a running story about the discovery of documents proving a vast conspiracy to promote obesity.

"How did the documents get to the papers?" Andrew asked with a twinkle in his eye.

I had to confess. "Well, Bud Miller joined CRAPO so I figured I might as well give him the satchel. CRAPO must have found some reporters who were interested."

Betty asked if I was still in touch with Bud.

"He can't be," Andrew interjected. "Bud was arrested trying to hijack a plane for CRAPO. Apparently he intended to drop leaflets all over the state capitol."

We all expressed surprise at not having read about that incident in the papers, but Andrews clammed up right away. I figured the Department of Homeland Security had Bud locked up in a secret prison somewhere.

We talked about how nice Sherlock's funeral had been. "Its awful they never found the body," Betty said sadly.

"Maybe he wasn't home when the place blew up," Andrew suggested. "Maybe he is not really dead. Has anybody seen him around?"

Betty kicked me under the table so I said nothing and the conversation moved on to CRAPO, whose membership had jumped dramatically after the naked corporate sleaze-balls were dumped in front of the newspaper building. The public exposure had motivated radicals from the labor unions to join CRAPO by the hundreds. Newspapers and politicians began calling for an investigation. At least two presidential candidates had declared reform of the food industry to be major planks in their platforms. The reformers were demanding extra high taxes be levied on high calories foods, that the food industry be forced to provide free treatment for eating disorders, and that they also should run anti-junk food ads for the next twenty years. The office of the president was still saying there had been no conspiracy, of course.

Changing the subject, Andrew asked me how the undercover investigation had turned out.

"They never did catch the thieves," I replied, "but the junk food stopped disappearing, so they concluded that the investigation had served its purpose. They seemed to be pretty satisfied overall. This way they did not have the expense of a trial or any adverse publicity."

We were all feeling pretty happy. We toasted each other for the roles we had played in helping the forces of Good triumph over Evil. But Andrew grinned at me. He knew I believed that the battle would never end. People who loved power and money would always be with us. They would rise to the top of all organizations because they had few compunctions about how they got there. And because these folks were in positions of power, big business and the government would periodically engage in shockingly immoral conspiracies. But hardly anyone was as cynical as I was about those things.

PART TWO

CHAPTER 1. THE BEGINNING

"I'm a populist who sounds like a socialist, but that does not mean I want a massive expansion of government programs. It means I think people should have as much choice as possible. Living costs should be kept low so that people can do something with their time besides work. It means I know corporations are not people and should be kept under control because they tend to be evil."

The man who spoke these words was standing on a podium in the local high school. He was surrounded by a quiet crowd. Most of them had attended to hear another candidate speak; they were just being politely attentive until this character got off the stage.

"I'm not a true socialist, but those guys can make a lot of good points. You folks out there might appreciate socialists too, if you thought about what they say with open minds. After all, socialism is frugal, a lot like Lutheranism."

Frowns were directed at him. This crowd did not like being described as having any socialist leanings.

"Socialists have more sense than Democrats," said the white-haired man. "The Democrats want every kid to get a four year college degree, which is wasteful and a lot less useful than training for job skills." He paused at this point. "After all," he chided them, "half the kids are below average in intelligence, despite all the claims their parents make to the contrary." The crowd rewarded him with a chuckle. He was right on that point. They knew they were guilty of being biased parents.

"The Democrats want a major new government program for developing renewable energy," he went on to say. "Developing renewable energy sources is very important, but socialists know that would involve the transfer of tax dollars to big corporations. The little guy will not benefit. Democrats want to rebuild New Orleans. A sensible socialist knows that big construction companies will end up with all the money. Democrats think that pouring money into laboratory research is accomplishing something; socialists know that death is inevitable."

The speaker looked around carefully. The crowd was listening to him now, so he spoke more forcefully.

"Democrats naively think the government can solve problems. Socialists know that our government is under the control of the capitalists. The most successful capitalists would sell worthless medicine to old people and unhealthy food to children. So every time we ask the government to do something, we end up screwing ourselves, because the big capitalists are calling the shots."

The audience stirred, getting excited in spite of themselves.

"Small is beautiful; big corporations and big government programs are not," the man said quietly. "We should pass laws that restrict corporate shenanigans. Repeal laws that restrict individual choices. Lower the cost of living so people can have a decent life without depending on economic growth. Reduce taxes, since most of the money goes out the back door in the form of corporate welfare. Affordable housing: use local zoning to force the contractors to build more town homes than big houses. Change suburban zoning into mixed land use so people can walk to work or school from their homes. Repeal regulations that limit use of light weight vehicles (tell me why bicycles can use the roads, but a golf cart cannot) so we can putt-putt around town instead of having to drive expensive vehicles and fill them with expensive fossil fuels."

He took a deep breath then continued.

"Put it all together, and here is the ten-point policy agenda we should be working toward. All of these things can be done with less tax revenues than we currently collect.

"One. Affordable housing, which we can accomplish by using the zoning powers we already possess at the local level.

"Two. Access to basic medical care, which we can accomplish by changing the licensing laws that prevent use of lower cost personnel and prevent delivery of services over the internet."

The speaker hesitated a moment, looking toward his wife, who sat in the front row, for encouragement. She nodded, and he continued.

"Three. Affordable transportation, which we can accomplish by eliminating the rules against cheap little vehicles.

"Four. Mixed land use; once again, we use our zoning powers.

"Five. Reduce taxes.

"Six. Low prices for goods services, accomplished by letting the corporations compete against each other.

"Seven. Regulation of corporations to prevent them from exploiting us.

"Eight. No legislation concerning matters that are personal and private."

Some of the people in his audience frowned at this point. He knew they were imagining what those hooligans in the big city would do if we did not have laws to keep their behavior under control. On the other hand, the same people did not want anyone telling them how to live their lives. This was indeed a difficult point for them to come to grips with.

"Nine. Reforming education so that schools provide job skills at an early age rather than postponing maturity. High school should end at the tenth grade, followed by vocational training or college depending on academic aptitude. Shift extra teachers from high school to grade school.

"Ten. And, of course, the government should provide security in the form of adequate police protection and guarding our borders."

He stopped to assess his audience. Had he given them too much information too quickly? Were they confused about the ten points? He decided to wrap up his message quickly.

"So, am I a Libertarian? Heck, no: Libertarians would let corporations run roughshod over the little guy.

"Am I a Republican? Heck, no: Republicans are like Libertarians, except they expect the corporations to give them highly paid jobs after they let the corporations run roughshod over the little guy.

"Am I an old-fashioned Socialist? Heck, no: those guys want the government to own the railroads, the utilities, and everything else that would otherwise turn a profit. I would rather let the capitalists run those businesses, regulate the heck out of them so they don't rip everybody off, and tax away a nice chunk of their profits. That way the little guy won't have to pay taxes.

"Am I Liberal? Heck, no: those guys want high personal income taxes combined with high levels of economic growth. They think everybody should live in a big house, drive a Volvo, and send their kids to Harvard. I might be a little nuts, but I'm not as crazy as an old-fashioned liberal.

"No, I'm just a populist. I believe that getting rich should be allowed, but it often reflects a certain moral degeneration in those who do it. Humility is a virtue and

141

flaunting wealth is crass. Frugality is a virtue and spending money unnecessarily is wrong because it is wasteful and self-indulgent.

The pursuit of thrills and excitement is trivial; a more appropriate goal is peace and serenity achieved through contemplation. This is a lesson most of us learn eventually, if we live through our youthful exuberance. Kindness is a virtue and exploiting other people to turn a profit is so wrong that it should not be allowed. And I believe that freedom of conscience and freedom of religion and freedom to choose how we live and how we spend our money is essential to having a good life. God bless America!"

The man with the white hair held up his hands as the crowd went crazy with cheers of enthusiastic support. He beamed as he reached out and shook as many hands as he could reach. But one of the hands he reached for held a gun, which fired directly into his heart. The man's happy grin changed to puzzlement as he dropped to the ground amid a suddenly silent crowd. Then a woman screamed and mass confusion ensued.

CHAPTER 2. WHO KILLED ED?

I sat up suddenly in bed, clutching my chest. My heart was racing and my body was dripping with sweat. Gasping, I rolled out of bed and staggered into the next room.

When I poured myself a glass of water, my hand shook, spilling out half of it. I gulped down as much as I could and refilled it. Then I sat down heavily in my Morris chair in the living room. Gradually, my head stopped spinning. Who would have expected that a dream about a political speech would have been so upsetting?

The sun was coming up before my heart stopped racing. By that time, Betty's alarm clock had begun its daily duty of trying to rouse her, so I started the coffee, showered, and dressed. Walking over to the convenience store to get the papers completed my recovery. By the time Betty was conscious, I was bringing her a donut with her coffee.

When she came out of the bedroom, dressed for work, I was munching happily on a donut.

"When did you get up? she asked sleepily.

"Just before sunrise."

"Why did you get up so early?"

"A dream woke me."

Betty was concerned. "You had a nightmare?"

"Well, sort of. I dreamed I was making a speech. It didn't go over too well."

"You probably upset people with your wild ideas."

"Yep."

"You're a curmudgeon, you know."

"Yep, I know."

"Where do you get all those ideas?"

"Maybe from thinking about religion. I was reading religious stuff almost all day yesterday."

"You weren't reading the Gospel of Thomas again, were you?

"Maybe."

"You'll go straight to Hell if you keep reading that stuff."

"Hell is separation from God. I'm not separated from God. Are you?"

Betty didn't answer. Betty had been raised Missouri Synod Lutheran, which meant that she was thoroughly programmed at her core that believing the 'wrong' way would send you straight to Hell with a capital 'H'. Thinking about theology always caused her to realize that she may not really have a perfect understanding of the Truth. Since believing wrongly led to damnation, thinking about theology was very frightening to Betty when she was little. As an adult, she had resolved the problem in two ways. First, she went to church and second, she never thought about theology. In fact, she generally didn't pay any attention to the sermon when she was in church. This is not as odd as it sounds, since Lutheran sermons are among the weakest in the known world. Lutherans select their pastors for their ability to carry a tune. Apparently the quality of a singing voice is inversely correlated with scholarly insight.

I should stop writing these observations right now or I might go straight to Hell.

Betty went off to work and I refilled my coffee to give my dream some more thought. Betty believed that dreams contained warnings. Since she was an anxious person, she thought danger was everywhere. Any clues to possible danger were to be taken seriously. Naturally, I could not have told her about my dream or she would have gone into a worry fit.

But I figured I should spend a little time trying to make sense out of it. Was it a premonition? Was someone going to shoot me if I did not control my outbursts?

Finally, I decided this was a silly way to think. After all, it was just a dream.

Having resolved that problem, I was free to spend the day however suited me best. You might be wondering why I did not go to work. Was I retired?

No, I was not retired. Well, not entirely. Occasionally an insurance company asked me to investigate some of its claims. Once in a while, I did some work for a private foundation, helping to spend its money for it. I even was called into the university now and then to function as a consulting ethicist.

But at this particular point in time, no one was asking for my services. So, I prepared for a day of fun and games. First, I hustled over to the nearest bookstore, the Velveteen Rabbit, to see if any new books had come in that looked good. The Rabbit was just the right distance for me to walk to, about half an hour through the residential neighborhoods. Next, I walked over to the library to see what was happening there. Then, I had to stop at the coffee shop down the street from the library for caffeine and a muffin. Then I walked home.

The afternoon was a little less exciting. I did the laundry, goofed around on the internet, and cleaned the cat box. By three in the afternoon I was sitting on the deck in the sun, smoking my pipe and telling myself how nice it was being semi-retired.

That's what you have to tell yourself when you have nothing else to do. You tell yourself you like the free time. You like not having a boss. You like being able to come and go as you please. And all of that was true.

The dark side of the situation, though, was feeling useless. No one seemed to care what I thought anymore. No one needed my skills very much. Maybe my skills were too rusty to be of much value. Maybe I was just plain obsolete. Maybe they should just take me out and shoot me. That was when I remembered that in a dream someone had done exactly that.

That evening, Betty and I met some friends at Sal's for dinner. Our downstairs neighbor, Emily Eberhardt, and Betty's cousin Andrew always were good for providing a stimulating discussion and a few laughs. Sal's was conveniently located and we like the ambience, so we went there regularly.

On this particular evening, a candidate for state senate came around shaking hands. She was a tall, beefy woman with a sincere smile. She introduced herself and informed us that she was the Democratic Party candidate for representative to the state legislature.

"Oh!" I responded enthusiastically. "That must mean you are going to fight corporate welfare."

The candidate hesitated, unsure of how to respond.

"What's corporate welfare?" Emily asked.

"Corporate welfare includes all the ways big corporations are able to get their hands on tax dollars, including subsidies, grants, and tax breaks," I responded.

Turning to our candidate, I asked her, "How are you going to put the brakes on corporate welfare?"

She gave me her best serious and sincere gaze. "I will work to represent all the people," she announced.

That knocked me back a little. "You didn't say you were against corporate welfare," I pointed out.

"I will represent all the people," she repeated, then moved on to the next table.

I nearly jumped out of my seat. "Did you hear that?" I demanded of my friends. "She's not against corporate welfare!" People sitting at the other tables turned to look.

"Sit down, Ed!" Betty demanded. "You're making a scene!"

"Sometimes it might be okay for corporations to get incentives, don't you think?" Emily was trying to play peacemaker.

I took a big breath then let it out slowly. "Emily," I asked her, "do you know the definition of capital, spelled c-a-p-i-t-a-l?"

Emily was a retired school teacher. I knew what her answer was going to be.

"Of course, I do. It's where the government is located. You know that, too. What's your point?"

"Capital also is defined as the wealth that is used in business enterprises."

Emily frowned. She knew I was right. Continuing with my argument, I asked them, "Have you ever wondered how business and government could be so intertwined that the same word represents wealth and the location of the government? It seems pretty darn obvious to me that big money has always been located with government. Heck, before modern governments developed, the kings controlled the government and also had most of the wealth. That is the natural order of things. If we don't fight it constantly, big money will always control the government."

My voice was rising again, since I was pretty upset. My face felt hot and my inflammatory remarks could be heard all over the room.

"But that particular politician is not going to stand up to big money. That tells me they already own a piece of her." I slumped down over my beer. "This is why I always vote third party," I growled.

Andrew had an answer for me. "If you feel so strongly about this, why don't you run for office yourself, instead of just complaining about it?"

"Maybe I just will, blast it! Somebody has to take a stand!"

Betty was shaking her head woefully. "You're getting to be a bigger curmudgeon every day," she moaned.

The next morning, I went over to the courthouse and filled out papers to become a candidate. The following week, the newspaper reported that the local League of

Women Voters was hosting speeches by three candidates for representative: a Democrat, a Republican, and an unknown Independent whose name was Ed Schumacher. The speeches were to be given in the high school on Monday evening, in less than a week. Remembering my dream, I wondered if I had less than a week left to live.

CHAPTER 3. ADVICE FROM THE WOLF

The dream was in the back of my mind constantly. Was it just a coincidence that I had dreamed about being a candidate immediately before becoming one? Of course not – the dream just showed my subconscious had been planning the move into politics long before the rest of me knew what was going on.

This made perfect sense, but it raised another question. If my subconscious accurately predicted that I would make a political speech, was it also accurate in predicting that someone would immediately shoot me? If it was right about the one, it could have been right about the other.

Only one course of action seemed possible to me. I had to assume that I would be murdered. Self-preservation demanded that I investigate the crime and solve it before it happened. If I did not investigate my own murder, I would not be able to prevent it. Off the top of my head I could not recall ever having heard or read about a person who had investigated his own murder before it actually happened, so the exact method for approaching this problem was a little bit unclear to me.

The dilemma was definitely surreal, so I resolved to consult with the most surreal person I knew. He didn't seem to have a name, so I just called him The Wolf. We occasionally had deep philosophical conversations outside at night, in a dark spot by the trash dumpster. The Wolf liked to be in deep shadow, so I cannot describe his appearance. However, based on a meeting with a colleague of his, I assumed The Wolf was a bit dirty, with long hair and a matted beard. Oh, and one other thing: his teeth probably were unusually large.

On the evening in question, Betty had gone to bed after watching her usual television programs. Near midnight, I gathered up my folding chair and my pipe, and took up my usual position by the dumpster. The Wolf might not come. Somehow, though, he always seemed to know I was out waiting for him, and he would manage to join me.

About half an hour after I was settled in my chair, I sensed a presence in the darkness. I said nothing, waiting for him to initiate the conversation.

"Nice evening, isn't it," he said.

"Yep."

We sat in comfortable silence for a moment.

"Hey, I have a question for you," I said. "Do you think dreams can foretell the future? Silly question, I know. But I'm curious as to what you think about it."

"How would I know? Sometimes I wonder if you aren't a bit superstitious. Like those people who thought they were hunting down werewolves last winter." Wolf chuckled, deep in his throat.

"Those were crazy folks, I know. Alright, forget I asked about the dream stuff. It was just a thought."

Wolf stirred out in the darkness. "Now you have my curiosity stirred up. What kind of dream are you talking about?"

I told him about the dream and also about how now I was a candidate for office with a speech scheduled in the near future.

"The real issue here is whether you are going to die after that speech, right?" Wolf was good at getting to the heart of a problem."

"Well, sure. That interests me. It would interest anybody."

"So what if you do? Nobody lives forever."

"Well, sure, but there is no need to go prematurely."

150

"Prematurely? If you really believe it was foretold in a dream, then it sounds like fate. You can't avoid fate."

"How do we know that? Maybe it's just a warning about what could happen if I'm not careful."

"What are your choices at this stage? You can give the speech or drop out of the race. If the dream is correct, then you die after the speech. If the dream is just a dream, then you don't die after the election. If you drop out of the race, then you will never know whether you were going to be shot. But you will know that you did the careful thing. What the hell, it's just an election. Why bother with it anyway? Why are you running?"

"Because some issues are important. People should be able to live a good life without having to work their butts off all the time. Some people want to try to get rich - more power to them. But other people have more sense and they should be able to live in a small place, cook their meals at home, and be comfortable."

Wolf didn't respond, so I tried to clarify my argument.

"Guys like you, for example, don't have regular jobs. By choosing to live without luxuries, you can still get by. But most people could not rough it out in the woods the way you do. They should be able to work the counter at the convenience store or maybe bag groceries and still live decently."

"Okay, I agree with all that. What's stopping them from doing what you say?"

"The cost of living goes up all the time. Builders build big expensive houses, but not many inexpensive places because there is less profit in the less expensive homes. The cars you can buy are mostly big, expensive gas guzzlers. Taxes are high, but a good share of the money goes to businesses that don't need it. Tax dollars support the schools, but people seem to take longer and longer to learn job skills. You should be able to learn a trade by the time you are 18, technical skills by the time you are 20, administrative skills by the time you are 22, and professional skills by the time you are 25. But we have young people graduating from college who still can't balance their checkbooks. Tax dollars are paying for all that education and the schools are not getting the job done."

I took a deep breath. "Both the corporations and the government have gotten too big. Both want people to work all the time so they can buy lots of things and pay high taxes. That makes us all slaves to the system. Am I making any sense to you?"

Wolf thought it all over for a few minutes then responded in a serious tone. "You're right, of course. People need the freedom to choose their lifestyles. Both government rules and economic pressures are eroding freedoms and soon it will be completely gone. People must speak up when they have the opportunity. You have the message and so you have a duty to throw it out for people to think about."

Wolf shifted his position. I sensed he was leaning toward me. "Ed, danger is part of life; a man of integrity must take chances. If you die, you die."

I laughed. "That's easy for you to say. You never give speeches. At least not in public."

He laughed in return. "Okay, I'm a hypocrite. But I'm not afraid to take my chances in life even though I know some day it will catch up with me. And different people have different gifts and different opportunities to use them. One thing you can do is talk in public; maybe more than you should. That's one of your gifts. I say, give the speech. The dream probably is just a dream, and if it isn't, then it's fate."

CHAPTER 4. ADVICE FROM SHERLOCK

Wolf's words bounced around inside my head for most of the next day. No matter what I was doing, they were never far from my mind. *Take a chance. Do what's right. If you die, you die.* Was that what it came down to?

My preference would be to solve my murder before it happened then prevent it. But where would I start? No one knew what I was going to say at the speech, so no one could possibly be angry enough to shoot me.

When your mind is stuck, take a walk. That was always my motto. So I strolled over to that fine coffee shop on Main Street, McDonald's, for a nice cup of black coffee. As I was sitting in the booth, blissfully sipping the brew, a man slipped into the seat across from me. I was amazed to see that it was my old friend Sherlock Holmes.

At this point a little background is in order. Sherlock and I had met while I was investigating a research project in my role as consulting ethicist. The project in question had studied psychiatric patients. The death of one of those patients had focused suspicion first on me, then on Sherlock. Sherlock Holmes was not his real name, of course. I am calling him that in these pages to protect his identity.

Sometime after the investigation of the research project, Sherlock somehow became involved in an organization calling itself CRAPO. CRAPO stood for Citizens Resistance Against Promotion of Obesity. They claimed that big corporations were deliberately promoting addiction to high-calorie foods, thus causing the worldwide obesity epidemic.

To make a long story short, Sherlock was now believed to be dead by most everyone, except me, and I was not altogether sure about it.

"Sherlock," I burst out with enthusiasm. "It's good to see you again."

He hung his head in that familiar way he had. "Yep," he offered bashfully.

"How long have you been in town? Or maybe you have been around, but just hiding out."

"I'm never far away."

"What have you been up to?"

He finally gave me a direct look. Sherlock had changed since I first met him. He had always been elusive and avoided confrontation at all times. He never argued with anyone. However, since the CRAPO business, he had shown flashes of strength and authority.

"We need to talk about what you're up to, not what I'm up to."

"Really?"

"You're scheduled to give a political speech on Monday."

"Yah, that's right."

"And you're afraid somebody might take offense at what you will say. In fact, somebody might get so mad that they decide to shoot you."

"How did you know about that?"

'Look, Ed. This ain't any of my business, but I'm a little disappointed in you. It ain't like you to chicken out when it comes to saying what's right. You never had to face the consequences in a serious way before, but now it's time." Sherlock stood up. "Part of your message is that corporations have to be kept under control. If we don't control them, they will sell us things that hurt us, get their hands on our tax money, ruin the environment, and make everybody work like dogs for low wages. Somebody has to stand up and point this out. We can't let corporations hurt innocent people without at least complaining a bit. Look,

ADVICE FROM THE WOLF

Ed. Don't keep your light under a bushel. You have to be brave sometimes. Death is not the worst thing that can happen to a person."

Then he left. I suspected he knew what he was talking about.

CHAPTER 5. MESSAGE IN A BOTTLE

The next day was Sunday. Betty was scheduled for hospital duty, so I was on my own. It was a great opportunity to review my life. Since it might be ending soon, reviewing my life seemed like a good idea.

First, I spent the morning reviewing some of my favorite religious books. Then, I went to church. My plan was to put myself in a truly spiritual frame of mind. Besides, church services have the effect of calming me down, and I was beginning to get distinctly nervous about my speech, which was scheduled for the following evening.

Lutheran church services are nice because of the litany and the music. Some of their features are a little difficult for us Protestants to get used to. (Yes, I know Lutherans think they are Protestants. Their services have a distinctly Catholic feel to them, despite all their protestations to the contrary.) One of the odd features of a Lutheran service is the practice of going up to the front of the room for communion. The hygiene aspects of it bother me enormously. And I hate waiting in line. But this practice has the merciful effect of shortening the time available for a sermon. As I mentioned earlier, when you miss a Lutheran sermon, you generally have not missed very much.

After the service, I made a fresh pot of coffee and settled into my Morris chair. The cats decided to help me with my ruminations. Bucky lay on his back in the middle of the living room floor with his legs in the air. That guy was no gentleman. Fritter sat primly upright with her tail curled around her legs. She was a lady.

At the top of a sheet of paper I wrote "My Contributions to the World," using a felt-tip marker so it would loom large on the page. Under the title on the left side of the paper I put the number 1 then leaned back in my chair to think. After about five minutes I was still thinking. Sometime after that, I must have fallen asleep, because when I woke up it was time for lunch.

I decided to try again. Taking my marker and my paper with me, I strolled over to McDonalds and parked myself in a booth. I resolved to put down anything I had done that might have some merit, and use a point system later to add it all up.

1. I had published a lot of scientific papers that nobody read. (This sounds self-critical, but the truth was most scientific papers are not read. So, I was not more useless than most people who had spent years in academics. If you look up the word academic in the dictionary you will find that it means 'irrelevant'. Those of us in academics were deserving of the name.)

2. I had taught students in graduate programs to do things that they could have learned in one-tenth the time, if we were more efficient. (But why would we want to be more efficient? We preferred to pretend that what we taught was extremely complex, when the truth was most of us didn't know what we were talking about half the time.)

3. I had solved management problems, thus helping to improve efficiency and effectiveness so that some consumers might have ended up getting lower prices and better quality. (The beneficial results of all these efforts were hard to prove.)

4. I helped to allocate the charitable funds of a private foundation. (This was really true and I enjoyed it, but it was also true that they could easily have done it without me.)

157

5. I donated money to charity. (The pennies they gave me in change at McDonalds went straight into the collection box for the Ronald McDonald house.)

6. I was kind to children. (I only was nice to them for a few seconds at a time and only if they were quiet; if they were noisy, I escaped their presence as quickly as possible.)

7. I was nice to my friends. (I decided not to make a list of friends. It would have been too short.)

8. I was a good husband. (I tried to be a good husband, but probably was not going to win any awards for it.)

9. I meant well in most of what I did. (Unfortunately, many of my well-meant efforts did not turn out as planned.)

10. I was nice to my cats. (There, I finally had found something I could get full points for. Of course, cats are easy. All you have to do is feed them, change the litter box, pet them when they want to be petted, and take them to the vet once in a while.)

11. I followed most of the rules we live by, including paying my taxes and my other bills, breaking very few laws, obeying the speed limit, not being deliberately cruel to anyone, and generally doing my 'duty.'

Adding all this up was depressing. If a human life can be scored from negative 100 (Adolf Hitler) to positive 100 (Mother Teresa), then I probably could give myself a number between zero and ten. I hoped he was not the kind of God who would send me back to live all over again until I got it right. That could take eternity.

Well, wasn't that just great? One more day to live was not enough time to gain many points. It was a good thing that I didn't believe a loving God would send anyone to purgatory or Hell after they were dead.

I folded up my list and wandered back to the condo. While I was walking, I remembered that we had finally emptied a bottle of port wine we purchased during the winter. We liked to have a little glass of port when we watched British mysteries on television. When I got back to the condo, I rinsed out the bottle. Then I wrote a letter to Betty telling her about the dream and the advice I got from Wolf and Sherlock. I told her I loved her and that I was sorry it had to turn out this way. Then I rolled up the letter and slid it down into the empty wine bottle, which I put back in its place in the liquor cabinet. If things turned out badly after my speech, Betty would eventually get into the liquor cabinet and find the letter.

When Betty got home we went over to Culver's since she deserved a treat for having to work on a weekend. While we there she asked me if we could go over to Michigan on vacation soon.

"Sure, why not?"

"Can we take the ferry across Lake Michigan?"

"Sure, why not?"

"Can we stay at a bed and breakfast?"

"Sure, why not?"

"You hate B&Bs."

"Just pick one that doesn't smell like flowers. And no bunnies on the bedspread."

"Okay! This is going to be fun!" She spent the rest of the evening online, shopping for B&Bs in Michigan. Betty was always happiest when she was shopping. And a happy Betty made for a happy Ed. I was going to miss that woman, if it is possible to miss anyone after you are dead.

CHAPTER 6. THE SPEECH

"My platform is based on Gospel, which I believe can legitimately drive policy without forcing any particular religion on people of different beliefs. Try this verse: 'Therefore I say, if the owner of a house knows that the thief is coming, he will begin his vigil before he comes and will not let him dig through into his house of his domain to carry away his goods. You, then, be on your guard against the world. Arm yourselves with great strength lest the robbers find a way to come to you, for the difficulty which you expect will (surely) materialize.' I take this to mean that we should be on guard against businesses that will exploit us if they can."

My speech had begun only a moment before this point. Since the two other candidates had gone first, my audience was having trouble focusing. Some were fidgeting and a few had already left.

I forged ahead. "Here is another: Jesus said, 'Love your brother like your soul, guard him like the pupil of your eye.' I take this to mean that our laws should protect people from harm. And we know that businesses will not worry about the well-being of their customers unless they have to, so we have to watch them carefully and make them behave." The audience was giving me blank looks. Was this a speech or a sermon? Was this guy a communist or a preacher?

"And let's not forget this one: Jesus said, 'You see the mote in your brother's eye, but you do not see the beam in your own eye.' Obviously, we all lack perfect understanding, so our policies should protect freedom of conscience so that each person can decide for himself what is right." That point got me a few nods. Maybe I was reaching them.

"The gospel also says: 'It is impossible for a man to mount two horses or to stretch two bows. And it is impossible for a servant to serve two masters; otherwise, he will honor the one and treat the other contemptuously. This tells me that people who pursue money and power cannot pursue goodness. We cannot change them, but we can try to keep them from running and ruining our society." People were waking up. The pitch was different, but what I was saying had a familiar ring.

"Most of us have better things to do than try to get rich. When asked 'When will the kingdom come?' Jesus answered, 'It will not come by waiting for it. It will not be a matter of saying 'here it is' or 'there it is.' Rather, the kingdom of the Father is spread out upon the earth, and men do not see it.'

"Those are the reasons I say we have more important things to do than amass wealth. Let the capitalists among us chase the almighty dollar, as long as they don't hurt other people in the process. If I am elected, I will enforce rules that limit the most outrageous corporate misbehavior. And I will keep the government out of our private and personal matters. I will pursue policies that will enable us to live well without constantly trying to make more money all of the time. That means having zoning and property tax polices that make housing affordable, giving our children basic job skills, assuring access to basic medical services, and controlling crime in our neighborhoods. I would keep government programs small so that we can control taxes; that will help to keep the cost of living low. "

That last point got a smattering of weak cheers. As I was leaving the podium a few people rose from their chairs to shake my hand. One of them had a pistol in his hand, which he fired directly into my face. Everything went black.

CHAPTER 7. CONCLUSION

The crowd had convened at Sal's, looking somber. Everyone was sitting around the table, glasses of beer in front of them. Andrew toasted Betty for her courage.

"Here's to Betty," he said. "For being brave despite having to witness Ed's assassination."

Everyone took sips from their beer.

Emily raised her glass. "And here's to Ed," she said. "Being shot in the face must have been very frightening."

Everyone took another sip.

Andrew had to put his two cents in at this point. "Sure it was frightening. But fainting dead away after being shot with a water pistol filled with ink is not going to get you many votes." The others repressed their grins.

I was not amused. "Does anybody know why the guy did that?" I demanded.

"The 'water pistol filled with ink' trick is a CRAPO publicity stunt." Andrew replied. "You remember CRAPO? That's the Citizens Resistance Against Promotion of Obesity. They like to get on the news with stunts like this one."

"Well, they certainly made their splash this time," Emily responded. Then she turned to me. "Ed, that was a fine speech. I liked the quotes from the Bible. But what version of the Bible were you using? That didn't sound like the King James Version to me. But it wasn't American Standard. So, what version did you use?"

Betty gave me a baleful glare. She knew the answer.

"Umm, Emily, those quotes were from a gospel that is not included in the Bible. It's called the Gospel of Thomas."

Emily was amazed. "Not included? I thought all the Gospels were included. Why didn't they include this one?"

"Because the early church leaders decided it was heresy," Betty burst out.

"Heresy!" Emily cried. She was a very religious person and this was a serious concern for her. "Why was it heresy?"

"Because the author apparently thought our essential beings are spiritual," I responded. "He probably thought our bodies stay behind when we die. That contradicts the Creed. He also left out the virgin birth, most of the miracles, and minor stuff like that."

Andrew was laughing. "You were quoting heresy in a political speech? Wait till the voters find that out! Ed Schumacher, the Fainting Heretic!" He laughed uncontrollably. "Ed," he gasped. "Somehow I don't think there is much chance you'll win this election."

We all had a good laugh. They were laughing at me, but I didn't mind. We had a good time.

When we got back to our condo, Betty decided to tidy up the kitchen while I sat out on the deck, smoking my pipe. As I was blissfully so engaged, she slid open the door, came out, and sat in the wicker chair next to mine. She held the letter I wrote to her in her hand. I had forgotten about that.

"What is this?" she demanded quietly.

"Well, you must have read it. But since I lived through the speech, there obviously was nothing to worry about. I was just being a bit hysterical."

"What you are is depressed."

"Depressed?"

"Yes, depressed. You don't have enough to do. And you feel like nobody needs you anymore."

"Hey, if I don't have anything to offer, that's just the way it is. I can't complain."

Betty reached across and grasped my hand. "Ed," she said earnestly. "You are a good man and you have lived a good life. Maybe you can't see that now, but you do plenty of good in the world. I know you are not world-famous, but you don't have to be." She took a breath. "Look, every person has to do the best he can with what he has to work with. When you do small kindnesses each day, you are putting a lot of joy into people's lives."

"Really?"

"Yes, really. Besides, I know you very well, and I know you are one of those people who tries to follow the rules. That means being honest, charitable, and humble. It means being temperate in food and drink and avoiding excesses of all kinds. It means worshiping in whatever ways work best for you."

"Do you think that is enough?"

"Of course, when you seem to have an opportunity to make a larger contribution, you volunteer, but it's okay if it passes you by. It doesn't make you *less good.* Few of us are destined to be brilliant doctors or to be compassionate nurses or to cure cancer. As for doing something wonderful that everyone applauds you for - forget it. Acclaim is not important. You are always railing about how bad it is to pursue money and power. Pursuing the limelight can be as destructive as pursing money or power."

"I agree. That's a darn good point."

"You are supposed to stand on principle even if there is some risk of being disliked or other more serious consequences. You can't expect everyone to agree with you or even to like you if you are telling the truth as you see it. On the other hand, you don't have to start an argument everywhere you go. Sometimes that seems like you are just trying to get attention."

"Ouch."

"Anyway, Ed, I just wanted you to know you are a good person. You make a contribution to the world, even if it is not something dramatic." Betty patted my hand.

"I'm sorry you're depressed. I don't know what to tell you, except 'snap out of it.'"

"Thanks. You're a very smart woman."

"You better believe it," she responded. Then she went back into the condo to finish cleaning up the kitchen, leaving me to ponder her wisdom.

From her perspective, by doing the best I could in small ways each day, I was doing enough good in the world. I should be satisfied that I was doing enough.

I felt better now. Not long ago I saw myself as already dead, but now I was alive. And I was getting closer to solving the mystery of life. Our goal is to reach peace and contentment. Sometimes, you can try too hard, and that pushes the goal farther away. Sometimes a guy like me just has to lighten up.

I went inside and walked over to Betty.

"I'll try not to be such a curmudgeon," I announced.

She smiled. "You do that dear. But if you slip now and then, I'll forgive you."

Bibliography

The Gospel According to Thomas. Selection made from James M. Robinson, ed., *The Nag Hammadi Library*, revised edition. HarperCollins, San Francisco, 1990. Downloaded May 7, 2006. from http://www.gnosis.org/naghamm/gthlamb.html

DEAD MAN'S BALLAST

This book is dedicated to all those portly and rotund individuals who try to control their weight, sometimes successfully and sometimes not.

CHAPTER 1. ED LEARNS TO FLY

The fresh coffee smelled wonderful as it bubbled its way into the pot. The first pot of the morning always smelled great. Since I was always the first one to arrive at the office, I always put the pot on. No, that is not entirely accurate: I made the coffee because I drank more of the stuff than anyone else.

While the coffee was making itself, I got my files in order. Since starting my new job as a weight loss coach, I had been very conscientious about it. Each of my scheduled appointments was a person who was serious enough about losing weight to make an appointment just to see me, so I took seriously my responsibility of helping them as much as I could. The family physician who was referring his patients to me was placing a lot of trust in a guy who had no formal credentials, so I was reviewing each patient's history carefully and thinking about the best way to approach each of them.

People were trickling into the office suite while I was making notes to myself for the morning's appointments. My job was only part-time so all the appointments were scheduled for the first part of the day. In fact, since my 'practice' was brand new, I only had four appointments scheduled.

You may be wondering how a guy with no formal credentials could be working as a weight loss coach. Well, that just shows how badly you have been hoodwinked by the obesity mafia.

Maybe that last statement was a little harsh. In fact, when I first decided I wanted to try weight loss coaching I approached several companies in our little town of Fort Atkinson, Wisconsin that were advertising vacant positions. The way they treated me soured me on the whole industry. My natural preference toward seeing weight-loss as a self-help business rather than a professional field was set in stone in just one day.

The first place I was interviewed at was a fitness center. The young woman who interviewed me was, as you might expect, very fit. She looked at me with a critical eye, quickly taking in my slack muscles and white hair.

"Mr. Schumacher," she announced. "I'm afraid there has been some misunderstanding. You are not the sort of person we hire for this kind of position."

"Oh, really?" I asked innocently. "What sort of person am I not?"

Translating that sentence required her to think for a few minutes. While she was working on that, I took note her of nametag. It said Sandra Coates.

"Ms. Coates," I went on. "I have a doctorate, years of experience in research, and, most importantly, I lost a lot of weight and kept it off. Those seem to be good credentials, in my mind. What are you looking for in an applicant?"

"Do you have experience selling fitness center memberships, primarily to younger women?"

"Uh, no."

"I'm not surprised. Younger women are more likely to buy a membership from a physically fit woman. They definitely do not want to buy a membership in a fitness center where older men have the run of the place."

Ouch.

"Okay, you have me there. I am not a physically fit young woman. But I thought this job involved weight loss counseling."

"It does. You counsel them to buy a membership in this club."

169

"But they need to eat less. Working out won't help them if they don't eat less."

"Are you an exercise physiologist, Mr. Schumacher?" Ms. Coates demanded.

"Uh, no."

"That's apparent. Thank you for your time. Good day."

And that was the end of that.

My next interview was for a position with a health food store. The manager, a somber woman whose name was Wilma Petersen, reacted to me in a similar way, but with a twist.

"Mr. Schumacher," she asked. "Are you a nutritionist?" She could tell by looking at me that I was still eating burgers now and then.

"No. But I'm sure you know that eating a balanced diet will not help you lose weight unless you consume fewer calories than you have been used to."

"That's true, Mr. Schumacher. Which is why we provide a special line of prepared foods, arranged in a well-organized sequence of menus for each day of the week. Do you think you could talk to our clients about the importance of special menus and our prepared meals?"

"Heck, no. They just need to eat less. They don't need to pay a lot of money for special packaged foods."

"Thank you for coming in, Mr. Schumacher. Have a nice day."

Finally, I was interviewed in a psychologist's office. The psychologist, Maggie Breedlove, was looking for a partner. She put me at ease with a smile.

"You are looking for a counseling position, Dr. Schumacher?"

"Yes, that's my goal."

"How is it going so far?"

"It has been an eye-opener. Somebody should investigate the weight-loss field. It's full of con games and shysters."

"You are right about that. In fact, I am so concerned about quality control that I am afraid I will not be able to retain your services. Your degree is in public health, not psychology. You do not hold a professional license. I'm sure you see my concerns. My hands are tied, I'm afraid."

"Wait a minute," I protested. "I can coach people about how to lose weight. There is no law against that."

"Dr. Schumacher," she said. "Counseling is a professional field. You need years of training in cognitive behavioral therapy. My patients come to me for months, sometimes years of therapy. You simply are not qualified.

"Years of therapy? A few tips and a pep talk is all they need!"

"Thank you for your time. Have a nice day." And that was the end of that."

Fortunately, for me, my doctor was supportive and he agreed to hire me on a trial basis to advise his clients. Even with his support, getting started was difficult. His nurse believed weight loss counseling was properly defined as 'patient education' and therefore only a registered nurse should do it. She hated me from the first minute I was there.

All that negativity was enough to get a person down. On the other hand, it would have been obvious to a blind man that each of the places I interviewed was taking advantage of overweight people by selling them services or products that probably weren't necessary and might not do them any good. That realization activated my stubborn streak and made me want to produce a group of satisfied customers who would tell the world that they had lost weight after a brief coaching session from a friendly guy with white hair.

My first client was a guy a lot like myself. I took a swig from my coffee while I looked him over. Wow, that was good coffee. It tasted so good, I immediately was confident that the session was going to go well.

"Mr. Schultz, I'm so glad you came in to see me. How are you doing today?"

"Just great," he responded. "It's going to be a nice day."

"That's always a good feeling, isn't it? Knowing that the weather will be nice?"

Schultz looked at me oddly. In retrospect, my remark sounded a little giddy.

"Well, what can I do for you today? Is there something I can help you with?"

"Well, sure. Doctor Wilbur said I should talk to you about losing weight."

"Be glad to. Do you think you need to lose weight?" Schultz's belly hung down well over the front of his pants. But unless he felt he needed to make a change, there was no hope of me helping him. Now was the time to find out. I took another sip of my coffee while he answered.

"Yah, I guess so. I used to be normal weight, about twenty years ago. Guess it sort of got out of hand."

"Do you think you eat too much?"

"Not particularly."

"What did you have for breakfast?"

"The usual. Bacon, eggs, hash browns."

"Well, I can see your problem right now. You need to cut that out."

"What?"

"Yes, sir. You drop that breakfast and replace it with just one piece of wheat toast. For lunch you have a dry crunchy granola bar with a big glass of water. In three months, you'll be a new man."

"That's all you have to tell me? That I should eat less?"

"Yep. That'll do it. Rule number eight for weight control is Eat Less. You can pay the lady at the desk on the way out."

"What about the other rules? Aren't you gonna tell me about them?"

"You may not need them. Number eight is the big one."

He looked disappointed, so I relented. "Okay, here is rule number four: Be Patient. Losing weight is a slow process, but it will happen eventually. If rules four and eight don't work for you, come to see me again. But keep at it. That ballast around your gut is going to make you a dead man."

Schultz got up, his face red. "Don't count on me coming back here," he growled, and marched out.

That went well, I congratulated myself. I refilled my cup and waited for the next client. That lucky individual was an elderly woman whose name was Matilda Federhoffen.

We went through the same routine regarding the weather, then I asked her what she had for breakfast.

"Half a grapefruit," she replied.

I leaned forward conspiratorially. "Mrs. Federhoffen," I asked. "Do you fix a nice dinner for your family."

"I surely do," she replied proudly.

"Mashed potatoes and gravy and pot roast and that sort of thing? With pie for dessert?"

"Yes, indeed. Nobody leaves my table hungry."

"Well, you better stop that."

"What?"

"Being exposed to all that food all the time is tempting you to nibble. You can't lose weight unless you get out of the kitchen. Tell those fat lazy slobs in your family that they are killing you by making you slave in the kitchen around all that food."

"Dr. Schumacher, I can't do that!"

"You have to. It's weight loss rule number seven: Engage Your Family. They have to support you. Let them do the cooking some of the time."

Mrs. Federhoffen left in a daze. I felt like a genius. My heart was racing and my face was flushed. I was so excited that I was jumping out of my chair.

173

My third and final client of the morning was a woman in her thirties. Her name was Hilda. She was pudgy but not excessively so.

"So, Hilda, you want to lose weight."

"Yes, I need to take off twenty-five pounds."

"Well, that's great. Goals are great. Making a commitment is weight loss rule number 3, as a matter of fact. Well, just take a nice walk every day. That will help."

"A walk? Don't I need to work out with weights and that sort of thing?"

"Nah, don't bother. Moderate exercise is weight loss rule number seven. The main thing though, is self-confidence. Just be confident you can take off those twenty-five pounds, and you will succeed. That's rule number two. And of course rule number five is to change your habits, like snacking less."

"That's all I have to do?"

"Yep. It worked for me. Do I look like a confident person?"

"You look almost giddy."

I guffawed loudly. "That's a good one! Giddy! Ha!"

Hilda got out of her chair to leave. She stopped at the door and asked, "Doctor, will you please tell me what rule number 1 is?"

"Well, I usually reserve that for special clients. But since you asked, I'll tell you. Rule number 1 is Empower Yourself. You need to adopt a philosophy that puts you in charge of your life. Don't let the food industry talk you into eating too much. Don't let your boss get you all stressed out. Don't buy too much stuff and end up with a lot of payments to make. That will keep you calm and in control of your life.

"How do I do all that?" she asked timidly.

"Vote third party. It works for me."

When Hilda left, I was too excited to stay in my seat, so I took the rest of the day off. Frankly, I was so jumpy I did not feel well at all. I stuck my head in Doc Wilbur's office and told him I was taking off.

"You feeling alright, Ed?" he asked. "You look a little wild. You're sweating."

"Maybe I'm coming down with the flu."

"Did you eat any breakfast?"

"Just a piece of wheat toast."

"Well, maybe you should grab a burger over at the Long Branch before you go home. You look a little peaked."

"Okay, I'll do that."

"And a Bloody Mary might be just the thing to help you take a nap when you get home."

"Okay, Wilbur. I'll try it."

Walking over to the saloon was like floating, I was so full of energy. They brought the Bloody Mary right away, and it boosted me up even more, so much so that I forgot I had ordered a burger.

The next thing I knew I was out in the bright sunshine in front of the saloon. The bridge that carried Main Street over the river was near by, and it looked beautiful so I wandered over toward it. Cars were honking, but I did not realize they were upset about how I had walked through traffic to cross the street.

Shortly after that, or so it seemed to me, my old friends Detectives Broder and Schmidt were talking to me.

"Mr. Schumacher," called Broder. He said it as if it was not the first time he had tried to get my attention.

"Yes, Bill. What can I do for you?"

"Whatcha doin' up there on the railing?"

He was right; I was standing on the concrete bridge railing. The surface of the water was far below me on one side.

"You know, Bill, that's a darn good question. You always were a bright fellah, I always said so. You always know what questions to ask."

"Why don't come down from there, Ed?" He was being very friendly.

"Why would I want to do that, Bill? The breeze is very cool up here. And I'm feeling very warm, for some reason."

Broder's partner was a mean female detective named Schmidt who had always been rude to me.

"Get your stupid tail down from there right now!" she demanded. "You look like a nut! Again!"

The woman was prejudiced against me. On the other hand, when was the last time I had seen anyone standing on the bridge railing?

"Well, you might have a point there," I replied. In fact, the world was starting to spin in a dizzying way. At that point, I lost my balance. Everything went black.

CHAPTER 2. ED WAKES UP IN THE HOSPITAL

When the world came into focus, I was laying in a hospital bed. My wife, Betty, was standing beside me. She was looking understandably concerned. Detectives Broder and Schmidt were lurking behind her.

"What day is it" I asked.

"It's Tuesday. You spent the night in the hospital."

"What happened?"

"You overdosed on allergy medicine," she replied.

After thinking back over my day as carefully as I could manage, I decided it was impossible. "Baloney," I said weakly. "Nine days out of ten I take an allergy pill. But the last few have been good. I haven't needed it."

"Lab tests showed you took at least half a dozen pills. You weren't trying to kill yourself, were you, Ed?" No wonder she was carrying around such a worried look on her face.

"No, I was not. And if that much stuff was in my system, somebody must have dissolved it into my coffee. I'm the only one who drinks that stuff at the clinic, so the culprit would have known I would be the only victim."

I pondered the problem for a moment.

"Hmm, Betty? Why would they give me enough to make me loopy? What would be the point of that?"

"Ed, you took enough," she corrected herself at this point, "they gave you enough to stop your heart. Most people would have gone right to sleep. They probably expected you to pass out on your desk and die on the spot."

"An out of shape guy my age…nobody would have been too surprised."

177

"That's right. If you had not reacted to the antihistamine by running around like a crazy man, no one would have been surprised. But since you acted like you were high on drugs, they dragged you in here and were able to stabilize you when your heart rate began to slow down."

"Why did it crank me up instead of putting me to sleep?"

"Because the medicine in your system was the non-drowsy kind. It was mixed with caffeine. And you drank coffee before you went to work, so your system was hyper-stimulated. Besides, some people react to drugs in atypical ways. Trust you to be different. In this case, it may have saved your life."

"Wow. Three cheers for being me."

"Let's not cheer just yet," interjected Schmidt. "You being you is probably why somebody put drugs in your coffee." Then she stomped out of the room.

Broder laughed. "Don't mind her. In fact, you owe her a big 'thank you'."

"Why?"

"Because when you passed out, she was the one who grabbed you and kept you from falling into the river."

Wilbur came around to see me, pronounced me fit to go, and told me to take a couple of days off.

"But I just started working at your office. Hey, you aren't going to fire me, are you?"

"No, but I have to be concerned about someone trying to kill you. Let's give the police some time to investigate. I would feel a lot better if they caught who did it before you started seeing patients again."

"Okay, I guess that makes sense. By the way, I'm afraid I may have upset some of those clients while I was high."

Wilbur laughed. "Actually, I saw Bob Shultz over at the Walgreens this afternoon. He was buying granola bars.

He said at first he was annoyed with you, but after thinking about it, he decided you have good horse sense. So, whatever you did, it seems to have motivated him."

"That's good to hear."

An hour later I was at home, sitting on the deck and smoking my pipe. My deck was really a balcony, since we lived on the second floor. The sun was out and the deck was protected from the breeze, so I was pretty comfortable up there. The cats were pressed up against the glass door, peering out at me and enjoying the way the sun warmed the glass. Bucky, the big cat, wanted to come out on the deck with me, but the big galoot probably would have jumped or fallen to the ground and then gotten lost.

My wicker chair had a wicker basket next to it where I kept my pipe and tobacco, and also a pad of paper and a mechanical pencil (medium lead). As I enjoyed the sun, I tried to figure out who was sufficiently annoyed with me to poison my coffee.

For the most part, my existence was pretty solitary. Betty and I went out with friends at least once a week, but my friends weren't the culprits. Occasionally, I did part-time investigative work for an insurance company, but I was not currently involved in a case. The only people I could think of whom I had recently crossed swords with were the weight-loss shysters. That included the woman at the fitness center, the woman at the health food store, the psychologist, and the nurse in Wilbur's office. The nurse obviously had the most opportunity, but any of them could have come into the office that morning without me seeing them.

So, I had suspects, but where was the motive? Being a competitor was hardly sufficient motivation for murder, especially since there was a good chance that customers would prefer to waste their money with the shysters than listen to common sense from me.

The puzzle was not solving itself, so I decided to take a break. A walk always sharpens my thinking, so strolled over to the grocery store to buy a loaf of wheat bread. While I was there, Maggie Breedlove, the psychologist, was loading groceries into the back of a Volvo wagon. She had purchased about a dozen bags of flax seed and an equal number of the large boxes of powdered milk. I couldn't resist going over to say 'hi'. After all, it was an opportunity to show there were no hard feelings about her not hiring me.

"Hey, Maggie. How's it goin'?"

"Fine. I hear you've started working in Doctor Wilbur's office."

"That's right."

"That working out okay for you?"

"The first day was a little rough, but Wilbur is satisfied, so I am hopeful that it will work out."

"That's nice. I wish you luck. It is a tough field to make a living in."

"Thanks for the good wishes. Say, I noticed all that powdered milk. The only time I ever needed that much powdered milk was when I was a teenager and my Dad bought me a bull to raise. I had to feed him a bucket of powdered milk every morning."

Maggie smiled. "Well, I'm thinking about getting a bull, just for fun. That's why I bought the milk."

We said our goodbyes and I went into the store to get my wheat bread. Frankly, I was confused. Maggie lived in a condo. Where was she going to keep a bull?

CHAPTER 3. ED AND BETTY GO TO CANADA

You may think that just about anybody could call themselves weight control advisors, as long as they didn't try to bill an insurance company for the service, and you would be correct. However, the more responsible quacks, such as myself, tried to prepare ourselves for the role. One of my efforts involved attending the American Psychiatric Association conference, which happened to be held in Toronto that year. My goal was to learn how over-eating was related to anxiety disorders, eating disorders, and addiction. Also, I hoped to learn how to recognize a person who might have a mental illness so that I could refer them to a qualified professional.

We drove to the meeting, since we avoided flying whenever possible. Our first adventure was the high-speed ferry ride across Lake Michigan, from Milwaukee to Muskegon. After that, the drive across Michigan was ordinary by upper-Midwest standards. If we had been from Nebraska or Kansas, we would have found it to be refreshingly green, but since we were from Wisconsin, we took the lush countryside for granted. We stopped for the night on the outskirts of Flint; that area did not impress us very much.

The border crossing into Ontario was effortless and the Canadian interstates were not that much different in appearance than those found in the United States. When we arrived in Toronto, the traffic became more congested. Streets were narrower than we had in Wisconsin, but not that much different than what you could find in New England. Fortunately, the drivers were polite and did not drive either too fast or too aggressively.

Even so, I was happy to disembark from the car when we finally found our hotel.

The conference was a disappointment. The eating disorders specialists were focused on anorexia and were not interested in ordinary over-eating. The anxiety specialists were not interested in over-eating as a consequence of anxiety. The addictions specialists only cared about alcohol and drugs. Apparently, psychiatry had decided that over-eating had no potentially serious psychiatric implications. That freed me from worry about running across psych cases among my clients, or it would have if I had believed it.

The lack of relevant presentations at the conference gave me an excuse to take several long walks around Toronto. It was a nice city, as cities go, but still traffic, hustle-and-bustle, and prices were all greater than small town folks prefer. One difference that I noted was the relative scarcity of large vehicles. In the United States, most people seemed to buy SUVs, pickup trucks, or large sedans, if they could scrape up enough credit to do so. Fuel efficiency was poor for all of the above. In Toronto, either public policy, narrow streets, lower incomes, or common sense prevailed more often, so people drove smaller cars. Betty and I even saw some of the fabled 'Smart cars', which were highly fuel efficient and commonly found in Europe, but never seen in the US.

A fair number of homeless people were in evidence. Toward dusk, you could see them staking out warm spots where they intended to spend the night. It was obvious that you needed to stay right on top of a warm spot or someone else would move in and take it over. Back home in the small towns of the Midwest, homeless people tended to be invisible; either they found a place indoors to sleep, or they moved to a bigger city, such as Madison.

Roaming around the side streets of Ontario on foot was good exercise, but it wore me out, so I stopped into a sandwich shop advertising toasted buttered bagels with coffee for $1.50. This was something I had not seen in the US, so I tried it. Turns out a toasted buttered bagel is exactly what it sounds like, and it tastes good as well as being inexpensive.

While my feet were recuperating and I was engrossed in my buttered bagel, my cell phone rang. It was Andrew.

"Ed. This is Andrew."

"Hey, Andrew. How are things back in the States? Cats doin' okay?" Andrew was watching our cats for us while we were out of town.

"Yes, the cats are fine. No problems there. But something else has come up and I wondered if you could help."

"Sure, but what can I do from up here in Canada?"

"A friend of mine at the office has a daughter who ran away from home. She called last night from a small town in Ontario, a place called Stratford. You might be driving through that area when you head back. If my friend can convince her to come home, can she ride with you?"

"Sure. I will check with Betty, but she won't have a problem with this." Even as I spoke the words, I began having second thoughts.

"Uh, Andrew? What's the story on this girl? She using drugs?"

"We don't think so. She has an eating disorder, gets very emotional sometimes, and seems to be very immature for her age. Heck, I don't really know how mature a 22-year-old girl is supposed to be. Anyway, she is legally an adult. Her name is Caroline, by the way. But she seems to have gotten involved with some guy she met at a party who took her on a wild road trip. She didn't tell her parents she was taking off. She didn't ask for time off work, so now she's lost her job. She cleaned out her bank account and has been running up her credit cards. Now that she's out of cash and her credit cards are maxed out, she and the guy are fighting. We figure he might just leave her and take off on his own, now that she is out of money."

"That's rotten. Okay, if she wants a ride, we'll take her. We plan to leave here first thing in the morning. We will plan to spend the night near Stratford, before driving into Michigan. If her parents can get her to come home, we will provide the transportation."

"Thanks, Ed. I will pass this along."

Betty had been attending the conference more conscientiously than I had. When she got back to the hotel that evening I explained the situation to her. She was willing to help out, but had a more realistic view of what we were getting ourselves into than I did.

"Caroline might be in pretty bad shape," Betty observed.

"Andrew said they don't think she's on drugs."

"Parents usually are surprised to find out about drugs. I would not be shocked if she is going into withdrawal when we pick her up. She might have been physically abused. She will be undernourished for sure, if she has anorexia nervosa. At a minimum, she will be an emotional wreck."

"Wow." I had not considered any of these possibilities. "You mean she might be bawling all the way back to Wisconsin?"

That was just the kind of insensitive remark that motivated Betty. "Yes, she might cry the whole way, and who can blame her? And you aren't going to complain about it one bit, are you?"

"Who, me? Not a chance."

When Betty and I drove through Stratford the next afternoon, we were struck by how many young people were wandering around the town. Stratford obviously was making some money off the Shakespearean connection. They had several playhouses in town and attracted tourists who were interested in plays. Presumably, some of the young people on the streets were aspiring actors and actresses.

Traffic was heavy and the general activity level was too intense for a small town fellow, especially after a long drive, so we went down the road to the next town, which was much quieter. We enjoyed a simple dinner of hot dogs and milk shakes at a drive-in,. After that, we were ready to quit for the day. A country inn looked very inviting, so we checked in.

The room we were given was located in the back of the building. It was private and very quiet. The grounds were beautiful. A bench just down the steps from our front door looked like a good place for me to plan to spend a few minutes the next day. At the moment, we just wanted to go to bed.

Betty went into the bathroom first. I was too tired to completely undress, so I just took off my shoes, fluffed up the pillows, and sat down on the bed to wait my turn. Betty could be counted on to spend half an hour getting ready for bed. I never did learn what she did during that half hour. Probably some things are better left as mysteries.

Speaking of mysteries, as I was dozing on the bed with my eyes half closed, my imagination got carried away and I saw a portly man in a gray suit just on the edge of my peripheral vision. I did not turn my head or even swivel my eyes in order to see him better, because of course, I knew he wasn't really there. He appeared to be quietly staring out the window, apparently oblivious to my presence on the bed. You may not believe this, but I was not worried, since I knew it was all my imagination. Besides, there was no sense of dread or fear. The specter seemed benign. Eventually, I drifted off to sleep.

When I awoke, Betty was in bed beside me. I was still fully dressed. Naturally, I got up and went into the bathroom. By this time, however, I was wide awake -still very tired, but wide awake- so I found my pipe fixings and went out to the bench for a smoke. The moonlight was bright and the air temperature, though cool, was not uncomfortable.

I took my time loading my pipe and lighting it. Then I leaned back a bit to enjoy the smoke. It was then that I noticed that a portly gentleman was sharing my bench with me. He was staring off into the distance, politely ignoring me.

"Nice evening," I offered.

He slowly turned his head and regarded me with a somber gaze. In the dim light his deep set eyes were shadowed, but his visage somehow communicated sadness. At the same time, the time it took for him to respond to my comment gave the impression that he seldom participated in conversations.

"Yes," he said. "Evenings here always are pleasant."

The silence that lay between us was not uncomfortable, but I had to ask the obvious question.

"Hmm, I don't mean to embarrass you, but by any chance were you in our room earlier this evening?"

A ghost of a smile appeared on his lips.

"Yes, I am afraid I should apologize about that. You see, I have been staying here so long that I tend to wander about at will. People generally take no notice of me. I hope I did not disturb you."

"No, I was not disturbed." It was true; the experience did not upset me the way perhaps it should have.

He nodded at my response, obviously pleased that he had caused no offense.

"What brings you to the inn," I asked.

He cocked his head to one side as he considered my the question. Apparently, he decided he could be open with me.

"I came some time ago to look for a dear niece. She had run away to Stratford."

"That's too bad. Have you had any luck finding her?"

His face grew even sadder. "No, I have never been able to find her. I fear I will have to look forever."

"You have my sympathies. As it turns out, we are here to pick up a girl who ran away from her home in Wisconsin. She was in Stratford when she called her parents a few days ago. If she wants to go home, we will take her with us when we leave."

The portly man nodded. "Very good of you." He appeared to ponder for a moment. "Perhaps that coincidence is why we happened to be on this bench at the same time. We may have been fated to have this conversation."

"That is an interesting thought. You might be right. If so, what conclusion or benefit do you think is fated to come out of our conversation?"

"Something perhaps to do with runaway girls?" he asked.

"I don't know what else it could be."

"It might be something else. What do you do for a living, if I might ask?"

"I'm getting ready for a new job as a weight-control counselor."

The man chuckled. "I should have met you a long time ago. It is too late now, I'm afraid. I know this ample paunch is deadly. I hope you are able to help some other poor soul to shed his surplus ballast before it is too late."

He shook his head in puzzlement. "No, I am afraid I cannot guess what it is that Fate intends me to tell you."

"Maybe I am supposed to tell you something."

"Yes? And what might that be?"

"Let me put it in the form of a couple of questions: How long must a parent, or an uncle, look for a missing adult child? How much rescuing are we obligated to provide?"

He was startled. "What are you getting at, Sir"

"Does rescuing sometimes postpone the day when a child grows into an adult? How can a child ever achieve

187

maturity if they don't suffer the consequences of their decisions?" I gestured toward the man with my pipe. "I know it sounds cruel, but the sad truth is that tragedy is a natural part of life. Sometimes our children make bad choices and suffer terrible consequences. Sometimes children suffer terribly even when they have done nothing to precipitate the problem. But, if the tragedy is not caused by the adults and cannot be prevented by the adults, then sometimes the adults have to recognize that they cannot correct the situation. Sometimes they must accept that circumstances are not under their control. They must forgive themselves for being powerless, get on with their grieving, and let go."

The man seemed to shrink and crumple lower onto the bench. I was afraid I had gone too far.

"I'm sorry. That was inappropriate, rude and insensitive. Please forgive me."

The man was silent for a moment. Finally, he said, "No, don't apologize. You have gotten my attention. This is why Fate put us on the bench together. I have stayed in this Inn long enough."

He stood up then offered me a stiff bow. "Good day to you, Sir. I will heed your advice. Take care on your travels."

He then walked out into the darkness with a dignified but purposeful stride.

Andrew called the next morning. Caroline was ready to go home. We picked up the cadaverous and ragged waif at a coffee shop in Stratford. Caroline slept most of the next day as we were driving. When we disembarked from the ferry in Milwaukee she started to become more animated and she and Betty had a good conversation. We were nearly back home, at the Johnson Creek exit, when Betty insisted I stop at the outlet mall. I knew she was intending to buy some decent clothes for Caroline to wear when she saw her parents. After they were done shopping, we went through the drive-thru window for ice cream at the Johnson Creek Culvers. I drove us into the village to the park, where we got out and strolled around while we slurped our snacks. Betty and Caroline seemed to have become friends. I didn't know how life was going to turn out for Caroline, but I knew that she would be better off having Betty for a friend. Betty would help Caroline in the future if she needed it and if she showed some appreciation. But Betty would not try to save Caroline from the consequences of every mess she got herself into. Betty was too wise to make that mistake.

CHAPTER 4. BUBBLE, BUBBLE, TOIL AND TROUBLE

Betty's cousin Andrew and I met at Sal's for a beer the evening after I got out of the hospital. He wanted to hear about the little escapade that led to me dancing on the bridge railing.

"So, Ed. I hear you are abusing drugs now."

"I deny everything."

"That's what they all say. Seriously, Ed. Betty is worried about you. She even thought you might have taken those pills on purpose. Sometimes she thinks you're depressed."

"That's ridiculous. Besides, why would I take pills that are full of caffeine to put myself down?"

"Anybody can make a mistake. You probably didn't know what was in them."

Andrew didn't really think I had tried to kill myself with allergy pills. He was just giving me a hard time.

"Well, I didn't do it. Instead of razzing me, you should be trying to help me figure out who would do such a thing to me."

"Who have you been annoying lately? There has to be someone. I can't imagine you would go through more than a couple of weeks without upsetting someone."

"I'm not involved in an insurance case at the moment. The only people I argued with were at some local businesses where I applied for part time jobs." I told Andrew about those interviews.

"Well, those folks don't sound like they have enough reason to try to kill you. Maybe if they had hired you they would feel that way, but since they didn't hire you, they're safe."

"Very funny."

"Well, I just wanted to tell you Betty was worried. In fact, she asked me to keep an eye you."

"That should be easy to do. I don't get out much. And I don't usually leave town."

"That's just as well. You'll get into less trouble that way."

The next morning I walked over to my favorite fine coffee shop, McDonald's, for a snack and a brew. As I was sitting in a booth, I started wondering why a psychologist would need lots of flax seed and powdered milk. Obviously, these were ingredients for something. But a dietician was more likely to need ingredients than a psychologist. On a hunch, I walked over to the health food store where Wilma Petersen was the manager. The store occupied a building in the retail stretch of Main Street, only about eight blocks from McDonald's. An alley in back provided access to all of the stores. I tried to be inconspicuous as I slipped down the alley and peered into the windows behind the health food store.

As is often the case, the back of the store was a stock room. The stock room contained a variety of health food items. And, by some strange coincidence, right in the center of the floor was a pile of newly arrived stock. I recognized the boxes immediately, since I just saw them an hour before as Maggie Breedlove loaded them into her Volvo. Now they were in the storeroom in the health food store. Why would that be?

I was so engrossed in peering into the stock room that I did not hear the pickup truck drive down the alley behind me. When the sound of gravel crunching caught my attention, I turned and saw Sandra Coates, the woman from the fitness center, getting out of the truck.

"Hey, Sandra," I said cheerfully, hoping she would not ask me what I was doing there.

She didn't. Apparently, she had figured it out all on her own. Deadpan, she asked me to help her carry some supplies into the health food store. I was happy to comply, since it gave me a chance to see inside the store. The supplies we carried included several cases of wheat germ, oat meal, graham cracker crumbs, jell-o and jell-o pudding. While we were stacking the boxes, Wilma Petersen joined us.

"Well, what have we here?" she asked.

Sandra waved toward me. "Ed was curious about what we have going on here, so I asked him to help me unload some supplies."

"Is that right?" Wilma replied. "Now what are we going to do with him?"

They were talking about me as if I was a piece of furniture. That bothered me a bit, so I spoke up.

"Hey, you guys. What's going on here anyway? What are you up to?"

Wilma and Sandra stared at me. Finally, Sandra said, "I guess we might as well tell him. He has seen too much anyway."

Wilma shrugged. "Okay, Ed. You might as well know." She obviously was pleased with the opportunity to brag about her cleverness. "What we do here is just good business, not that we want anyone to know. First off, Sandra at the fitness center, Maggie and I have this little referral arrangement. I encourage most of my patients to go join the fitness center and see Maggie for psych counseling. They refer to each other. And everybody pushes their clients to buy our diet food. Maggie, Sandra and I are partners in the diet food business, which is where we make our real money."

"Is the nurse over in Doc Wilbur's office in your little club?"

192

"Why would you think that, Ed? You must be as paranoid as people say you are. No, it's just the three of us. But now that you mention it, she would be a good addition to the group. She can refer a lot of customers our way. Thanks for the tip. We will check her out to see if she can be recruited.

I looked around the store room. "You mix this stuff up to make meal substitutes, then slap a name brand on it and charge a high price."

"Very good, Ed," Wilma said, obviously pleased that I had finally figured it out. "People can buy our milk shakes either in cans or in boxes, in powdered form. We make them out of cheap ingredients. After all, the idea is just to make the person feel full without giving them a lot of calories. With the right amount of artificial sweetener and some flavoring, anything tastes pretty good. Good enough to be diet food, anyway."

"That's pretty clever," I admitted. "But why not just sell a cookbook instead of making counterfeit diet food? You could go to jail for doing this."

"Ed, for a smart guy you can be pretty dumb. The profits are much higher when people think they are buying something special. If you tell them it's something they can do for themselves at a low cost, they think it's too easy. That's why your self-help coaching business is never going to work as well as our diet food business."

"Say, that reminds me," I burst out. "You guys must have poisoned me. Why did you do that if I could not possibly offer a competitive threat to your businesses?"

"You don't offer a competitive threat, Ed. But you were talking about an investigation when you interviewed for the job Maggie is trying to fill. An investigation could have been disastrous for us. In fact, we were expecting you to turn up eventually, since you have a reputation for digging into investigations until you solve the puzzle. We heard you settle your cases mostly through luck, rather than skill, but we couldn't take a chance that you might stumble on the truth." She smiled. "And it turns out we were right to be concerned, because here you are."

"Well, ladies, the jig is up. I'm calling the cops."

Sandra laughed. "Are you, really, Ed? You would have to get past me to do it.

Sandra was a fitness instructor. She was bigger than I was and she had genuine muscles. She probably had muscles where had I never had muscles, even when I was thirty years younger.

I decided not to try to get past her. The two of them were giggling when they locked me into the stock room.

CHAPTER 5. TRAPPED!

This was a fine dilemma, I told myself. Trapped by murderous diet freaks. Only they weren't genuine diet freaks; they were frauds and shysters. Unlike myself, who was just a harmless quack. Quacks obviously were superior to frauds and shysters. And to prove it, I had to figure out a way to escape from this room and bring the low done on the gang of murderesses.

Five hours later I was still working on that. I tried applying the rules for weight control to my problem. This was certainly a good situation for applying the basic principles of Self Help, Self Care and Self Confidence. Unfortunately, the door was locked and the windows were barred, so I could not help myself and my confidence had completely eroded.

However, an insight had occurred to me. People with eating disorders, such as our young friend Caroline, could be seriously harmed by scams such as the one being carried out by my captors. If your goal is to sell as much diet food and as many weight-loss services as you can, then you might regard a person with an eating disorder as a good customer rather than as someone you should refer to a doctor for treatment that encourages her to eat more rather than less. It sounded to be like the diet industry was like the liquor industry: bartenders only cut off the customers if they got into fights or were too drunk to drive. What would a customer have to do to be cut-off by a diet food store?

The national preoccupation with obesity was a good thing and it was important. But if we weren't careful, we

195

were going increase the number of people who had the opposite problem. The goal we had to promote was not being as thin as possible, but simply reaching a reasonably moderate balance. Either extreme, eating too much or eating too little obviously was bad for you. Obvious or not, some people were at risk for falling into either one of those extremes. From now on, my message was not going to be 'lose weight'. Instead, I was going to push moderation. I was not sure I could make a living that way, but it was the only responsible way to behave.

Around midnight, the door opened and standing in the entrance were Detective Broder and a couple of uniformed patrolmen.

"You guys are a sight for sore eyes!" I exclaimed. "How did you find me?"

"Your friend Andrew called us when you didn't show up at your home tonight," Broder replied. "The counter guy at McDonald's saw you this morning and a couple of store owners reported a suspicious person lurking in the alley just after that. We put two and two together and came up with you. After that, it was just a matter of knocking on doors until we found you. Andrew said you were suspicious of the health food store manager, so we insisted that she give us a tour. She tried to run, which was a dead giveaway. She's down at the station now. Schmidt is interrogating her."

"Ouch, I know how that feels. I almost feel sorry for Wilma. I bet she's spilling her guts about now."

Broder laughed. "I wouldn't be a bit surprised," he said. Then he turned serious. "Ed, when are you going to learn to stay out of the investigating business and leave it to the professionals?"

"Are you telling me that you guys were about to find out who had poisoned my coffee?"

Broder acquired a pained look on his face, but he didn't answer my question. We both knew they had made no progress solving the case.

"Well, then, maybe I should just keep investigating cases when they come up, since you guys appear to need some help solving them."

"Ed, you keep doing that, and someday you are going to get into a situation we can't get you out of. This time we could have ended up finding your DNA in a jar of health food. Doesn't that scare you, at least a little bit?"

"Sure it scares me, Bill. But a man's gotta do what a man's gotta do." My response sounded weak, even to me. But, as time goes by, it sounds more and more like a rule to live by.

APPENDIX: RULES FOR WEIGHT CONTROL (AND EVERYTHING ELSE IN LIFE TOO)

1. Philosophy. Empower yourself by adopting a personal philosophy that endorses non-material values. Don't let our society push you into stressful jobs and a high debt load.

2. Confidence. Recognize that many people have succeeded in losing weight and making other important changes in their lives. If they can do it, you can do it.

3. Commitment. Sign a contract with yourself and your family. The contract is a serious obligation. It means that controlling your weight is a priority. It is more important than trivial matters like whether you prefer regular soda to diet soda. It involves a permanent change in lifestyle, rather than a temporary diet.

4. Patience. Recognize that permanent weight loss is a slow process. Be comfortable with the pace of change, secure in the confidence that even if it takes two years to lose the extra pounds, you will enjoy being a healthy weight for the rest of your life.

5. Change your habits. Be alert to situations in which you get the munchies. Avoid those situations. Find something else to do. Sit somewhere else. Take a walk. Drink a glass of water. Find a hobby you really enjoy and immerse yourself in it. Surround yourself with motivational reminders.

6. Engage your family. You need family support to make the changes in lifestyle that are necessary. Even more important, you need your family not to undermine your weight-control efforts. They may not realize they are a danger to your waist-line, so you may have to teach them that the demands for snack food and large meals are

insensitive to the weight problems of some family members. Besides, if they continue to consume calories in large quantities, the rest of the family will become obese as well.

7. Moderate exercise. Walk a mile or two most days of the week or engage in some other kind of exercise. You will feel a lot better if you do. For many of us, having a destination is easier than walking for exercise, so plan your walks so that you are going somewhere, even if it is just to a coffee shop.

8. Eat lightly. This, of course, is the most difficult attitude change. We are not depriving ourselves if we eat small quantities. After you adjust to the change, you can become quite satisfied with light meals.